Chestnut Hill

Playing for Keeps

Also by Lauren Brooke:

Chestnut Hill
The New Class
Making Strides
Heart of Gold

The *Heartland* series

CH

Chestnut Hill

Playing for Keeps

Lauren Brooke

SCHOLASTIC

With special thanks to Catherine Hapka

First published in the US by Scholastic Inc., 2006
This edition published in the UK by Scholastic Ltd, 2007
Scholastic Children's Books
An imprint of Scholastic Ltd
Euston House, 24 Eversholt Street, London, NW1 1DB, UK
Registered office: Westfield Road, Southam, Warwickshire, CV47 0RA
SCHOLASTIC and associated logos are trademarks and or registered trademarks of Scholastic Inc.

10 digit ISBN 0 439 95133 X
13 digit ISBN 978 0439 95133 3

British Library Cataloguing-in-Publication Data.
A CIP catalogue record for this book is available from the British Library

Printed in the UK by CPI Bookmarque, Croydon, CR0 4TD
Papers used by Scholastic Children's Books are made from wood grown in sustainable forests.

7 9 10 8 6

www.scholastic.co.uk/zone

Chapter One

"Earth to Lani. Focus, cowgirl!"

Lani Hernandez blinked. "Huh? Oh, sorry, Dad. I was just trying to figure out how much longer it'll take to get to Chestnut Hill. What were you saying?"

"I was asking if you're planning to finish your dessert or just sit there staring at it," her father quipped with a twinkle in his brown eyes. "We need to get back on the road soon if we're going to stay on schedule."

Lani glanced down at the last bite of chocolate cream pie on the plate in front of her. "I don't know if I can finish – I'm stuffed," she admitted, leaning back from the diner's Formica counter and holding her stomach.

Her father reached over and scooped up the pie with his fork. "Living out east is making you soft, *chica*."

Lani grinned. "Oh, yeah?" she challenged. "Come watch me wrestle with Colorado when he decides he'd rather go back to his stall than stay in the ring. Then we'll see if you think I've gone soft!"

With a shiver of excitement, Lani realized she'd be

back on the campus of her boarding school, Chestnut Hill, in less than an hour. She couldn't wait to see her favourite school pony, a sometimes-tricky buckskin named Colorado – not to mention her best friends Dylan, Honey, and Malory, and the rest of the girls from her dorm. She had missed them all like crazy over the winter holiday break, even though it had been great spending time with her family in Colorado Springs.

Her father drained his coffee cup, then turned to summon the waitress. Lani took the opportunity to study his familiar profile. Strong chin, hawklike nose, intelligent brown eyes...

Sometimes Lani thought being in a room with her family was like looking into one of those endlessly repeating fun-house mirrors – one set of laughing brown eyes after another. While Guadeloupe, the second-oldest sister, had inherited their mother's blonde hair, and her other sisters, Marta and Dacil, shared Mrs Hernandez's petite height, all four of the Hernandez girls had their father's eyes.

"Ready to go?"

Lani realized her father was pulling on his coat. "Sure," she said. "Let's hit the road."

Grabbing her new Mountain Horse winter jacket – a Christmas gift from her grandparents – Lani followed her dad towards the exit. Stepping outside felt like walking into a freezer after the overly warm, grease-and-coffee-scented atmosphere of the bustling roadside diner. She shivered and zipped up her jacket, but her father didn't seem to notice the cold. Even with her long legs, Lani had trouble keeping up with his brisk stride as he headed toward their rental car, a large beige Buick sedan that Lani had nicknamed the Titanic.

"Wait up," she panted, breaking into a jog. "This isn't some Air Force march, you know."

Her father glanced over his shoulder. "Sorry, cowgirl," he said, slowing slightly. As the only member of the Hernandez family with a passion for horses, plus a particular interest in Western riding, Lani was more than used to her nickname. "It's just that lunch took a little longer than I'd planned. And I still need to make the long drive back to DC."

After dropping her back off at school, Lani's father would be spending the next two weeks in Washington, DC. As a commander in the US Air Force, his job regularly took him from his current base in Colorado Springs to the nation's capital and various other spots around the country. Lani's mom was a florist, and ran a successful store in the centre of Colorado Springs that specialized in wedding displays. Both their jobs depended on staying on a tight schedule, and Lani was used to living by a strict timetable – even when she would have preferred to stop and smell the roses.

Soon they were pulling back on to the highway. The radio was playing quietly, tuned to a local country music station. Kenny Chesney's soft drawl poured out of the speakers, and Lani reached over to turn it up, humming along.

"I'd better not let the girls from school find out I was listening to this," she joked. "I've already got a rep as some kind of hick for wearing chaps instead of johdpurs." She smiled, picturing the look of distaste Lynsey Harrison got on her face whenever Lani appeared in her beloved chocolate-coloured split-cowhide fringed chaps. "I don't think Dylan and Razina and some of the other New Yorkers even knew country music existed until they came to Virginia," she added with a grin.

Her father didn't answer. Lani glanced over, wondering if he'd heard her. His gaze was trained on the road ahead and his hands gripped the wheel at ten and two.

"Dad?" Lani said.

"Hmm?" He met her gaze briefly before returning his eyes to the road. "Sorry, Lani. Did you say something?"

"It doesn't matter." She leaned back and fiddled with the buckle of her seat belt. Normally she loved spending time with her father. Between their big family and his busy job, it was rare to have him all to herself for more than about thirty seconds at a time.

But so far, this trip hadn't been quite the fun-fest she'd expected. Everything had seemed normal enough on the flight to Boston, when her sister Marta had been with them. But after they'd dropped Marta off in her dorm at BU, things started to get weird. Not big-time, *Invasion of the Body Snatchers* weird – just weird enough to make Lani worry. Her father still laughed at her jokes and rolled his eyes at her near-constant references to Colorado and the other horses at

Chestnut Hill, but something still felt ...*different*. He seemed distracted, a little reserved. As if they'd argued recently and were being careful with each other, even though they hadn't had so much as a squabble over the holidays.

I bet most people wouldn't even notice he was acting weird, Lani thought. *But he is. And I have no idea why...*

Biting her lip, she reminded herself that wasn't exactly true. She had an inkling of the reason. She just preferred not to think about it.

She stared out the window at the Virginia countryside. Back home in Colorado Springs, there were a couple of feet of snow on the ground, and in Boston they'd had a few inches fall only the night before. But here everything just looked cold, brown, and brittle, from the frost-killed grass to the bare branches of the trees lining the highway.

"Wow, it sure looks different here now than it did in the autumn," she commented, remembering the way the -campus trees had burst into a glorious display of orange, gold, and crimson foliage soon after the start of the last term.

Her father nodded. "That's Virginia for you – the worst of both worlds. Too hot in summer, and too cold in winter. Bet it makes you wish you'd decided to go to boarding school in California like your sisters, doesn't it?"

It was a familiar joke, but Lani noticed her dad didn't crack a smile this time.

"No way," she said lightly. "They might have the

awesome weather out there in Cali. But remember, Chestnut Hill has one much more important thing their school doesn't have."

"I know, I know. The best horseback riding programme in the free world, right?"

"Got it in one! I taught you well."

She grinned at him, and he turned to smile at her briefly. But instead of launching into one of his playful speeches about how horseback riding wasn't *really* a sport or his famous, ever-changing, and always-hysterical list of the "101 most annoying things about horses," he merely turned away and started fiddling with the car's heater.

They drifted off into silence again. Lani couldn't help feeling tense. She tried to tell herself that her father was probably just distracted by all the work he had to do next week, or maybe he was worrying over the drive back to his hotel through the insane late-afternoon DC traffic. But she couldn't quite convince herself.

Let's face it – he's got to be thinking about my report card, she admitted grimly. *So why doesn't he just say so?*

Her stomach did a sudden flip-flop of anxiety. The one dark spot in her otherwise incredible first term at Chestnut Hill had arrived in the mail a few days after the start of the holiday break. When she'd torn open the report card, she'd been shocked to find only two A's – in maths and phys ed – with the rest of her marks falling between B-pluses and B-minuses. For some people, that might have been considered an excellent performance. But Lani was used to getting straight A's in all her subjects, and A-pluses in maths and science.

Maybe I shouldn't have spent so much time at the stable last term, she thought, twisting the seat belt buckle in her hands. *Or hanging out with my friends. Or helping Malory and Dylan and the rest of the junior jumping team get ready for their shows. Or picking out costumes for the Halloween Dance. Or practicing plaiting Colorado's mane. Or trying to play cupid with Malory and Caleb. Or about a million other things...*

Lani sighed as she thought back over her busy first term at Chestnut Hill. It had been a lot of fun, but it hadn't left much time for studying. She'd never had any trouble making straight A's before, no matter how many extracurriculars she took on, and so it had been a shock to find that she might actually have to put in some effort if she wanted to keep up with Chestnut Hill's rigorous academic programme.

I still can't believe Mom and Dad didn't say anything to me about my marks over the break. Still, it's just as well, she told herself with renewed determination. *Because it's never going to happen again. This term, I'm going to buckle down and bring those marks right back up to where they should be. Problem solved.*

"Check it out, Dad," Lani cried, pointing. Her face was pressed to the glass as the car joined a line of traffic making its way up Chestnut Hill's long, sweeping, oak-lined drive. They eased to a stop beside a painted white post-and-board fence. Behind it, a handsome dapple-grey gelding was watching the cars go by, his ears pricked forward. "That's Quince. He's Ms Carmichael's horse."

Her father glanced toward the paddock. "Whose horse?"

"Ms Carmichael," Lani repeated. "You know – Ali Carmichael, the Director of Riding. She's also Dylan's aunt. I told you about her, remember?"

"Mmm."

Before Lani could figure out whether his "mmm" meant "yes" or "no," the line of cars started moving again, creeping along bumper-to-bumper as the drive curved to the right. The stable area dropped out of sight, replaced by an impressive view of Old House, the imposing colonial building that was the campus's centrepiece. A few minutes after that, they were finally turning onto the road that led off to the dorMs

"Let's just dump my stuff upstairs and then go straight down to the stable," Lani suggested as her father pulled up in front of Adams House, her dorm. "I really want you to meet Colorado." She grinned. "I'm sure you can't wait to lay your eyes on the stunning specimen of equine magnificence I've been telling you about for the past three weeks."

Her father glanced at his watch. "Sorry, Lani, but I'll have to take a rain check," he said. "I need to get back on the road as soon as we unload your bags."

"What?" Lani's father was already climbing out of the car, so she quickly unhooked her seat belt and hopped out as well, squinting across the car roof at him in the bright afternoon sun. "But I thought you'd want to see everything. Especially the stables..."

"Sorry. Not this time."

Lani opened her mouth to argue, but snapped it shut again without speaking. Once her father made up his mind, usually there was no changing it. Most of the time, that didn't stop her from trying, but this time she wasn't sure it was worth it. Did she really want to finish up their time together with a big argument, especially when things already felt so weird between them? She gnawed on her lower lip, wondering what to do as she watched him march around toward the trunk of the car.

"Yo, Hernandez!"

Lani forgot all about her dismay at the sound of the familiar voice. "Dylan!" she shrieked, turning around just in time to get bowled over by her friend's hug.

"I thought you'd never get here," Dylan exclaimed, pulling back and shoving a stray lock of red hair out of her face. "The others have been back for ages. We were starting to think you dropped out or something!"

"Never," Lani declared. Noticing her father watching them, she waved him over. "Hey, Dad, this is Dylan Walsh," she said. "She's one of my—"

"Best friends," he finished for her. "Yes, I know. You only mentioned her name nine hundred and twenty-seven times over the past three weeks."

Dylan grinned. "Nice to meet you, Commander Hernandez," she said. "I feel like I should salute or something, but I don't know how."

Lani's father chuckled. "At ease, Private," he said.

"Very nice to meet you, too. Now, I understand you're quite a rider. But how do you feel about playing packhorse?"

"Load me up," Dylan said gamely, reaching for the duffel bag he had just taken out of the trunk.

Soon the three of them were trudging up the steps toward the dorm room Lani shared with Malory O'Neil and Alexandra Cooper. Lani was leading the way, with Dylan right behind her.

"Geez, this shopping bag weighs a ton, Lani. What do you have in here – the Colorado Rockies?" Dylan complained breathlessly. "Or maybe a few new pairs of boots?"

"Yeah, I figured I'd bring back enough cowboy boots and chaps for the whole riding class," Lani joked. "Your boots are two-tone teal and black ostrich – they just screamed Dylan."

Dylan laughed. "I almost wish you were serious," she said. "Just for the chance to see Lynsey's and Patience's reaction. They would probably gag in unison."

Soon the convoy was pushing through the half-open door of Lani's room. Lani was still hoping her father might change his mind and stick around for a while – at least long enough to walk down and see the stables. But she'd barely set down the bags she was carrying when her father checked his watch again.

"Sorry to cut this visit so short, ladies," he said, "but I really need to get back on the road. Are you all set, Lani?"

"Sure, Dad." Lani bit back her disappointment as she

stepped toward him. "Thanks for driving me down. It was fun hanging with you."

"You, too, cowgirl." The corners of his eyes crinkled as he smiled. For a second, he looked just like his usual self. "Now come on and give your old man a hug before I go."

"Is that an order, Commander?" Lani teased.

"Yep! Now step lively, Private."

Lani threw her arms around him, holding her breath as he squeezed her tightly in return. Even though she was happy to be back at school, she couldn't help feeling a pang of homesickness, knowing it would be a couple of months before she got the chance to hug him like that again.

"I'll miss you," he whispered, his warm breath tickling her ear.

"Me, too," she whispered back, feeling the knot of worry she'd nursed throughout the long drive loosen a little.

Maybe Dad really is just distracted by work, she thought as she breathed in the familiar, spicy scent of her father's aftershave. *If he were worried about my marks, he'd say so. But I'm still going to make absolutely sure I bring home straight A's this term – just in case.*

Chapter Two

"OK, first things first," Dylan announced, flopping onto her bed and sending several piles of clothes flying. "Inquiring minds want to know, Mal. How many times did you get to hang out with Caleb over the holidays?"

Lani had been standing at the window of Dylan and Honey's dorm room waving goodbye as her father's car pulled away. But now she turned around, glancing curiously at Malory.

"Yeah, let's hear all the dirt, O'Neil," she urged.

"Please," Honey added, glancing up from sorting through a large suitcase.

Malory was sprawled on the floor near Honey's bed, her long legs propped up on an open dresser drawer. She had immediately started blushing at Dylan's question, and Lani exchanged an amused glance with Honey. Caleb Smith was an eighth-grader at neighbouring Saint Christopher's Academy, more commonly known as Saint Kits. He and Malory had met at a local stable the summer before, and seemed well on the way to becoming more than friends. They'd even gone on their first date toward the end of the previous term – a rather overcrowded group gathering at a local coffeehouse.

"I saw him a few times," Malory admitted, sitting up and picking at the edge of Honey's bedspread. "Mostly at the barn, of course. But the best time definitely had to be when we went to a local jumper show together."

"Sounds like a date to me," Dylan said, waggling her eyebrows suggestively. She sat up and perched at the foot of the bed, staring at Malory.

Malory held up her hands. "Don't get carried away," she warned. "I wouldn't go around calling us boyfriend and girlfriend yet."

"Yet?" Lani accused. "Did you just say *yet*?"

Despite her joking tone, Lani's heart jumped a little on Malory's behalf. Lani had plenty of guy friends back home in Colorado – she'd always got along with boys just as well as she did with girls. But she'd never had a boyfriend or even a serious crush. That didn't mean she wasn't interested in romance, though – especially when it came to matchmaking for her friends.

Picking up a stray bedroom slipper, Malory winged it at her. Lani ducked and the missile missed her completely, bouncing off the windowsill and disappearing behind the room's third twin bed, which was piled high with monogrammed cognac leather luggage. The owner of that luggage, Lynsey Harrison, hadn't made an appearance since Lani's arrival.

"Hey!" Dylan cried in mock anger. "Watch it, Malory. You're going to mess up our room."

Nobody could keep a straight face at that, including Lani. Adams Room Two looked as if a tornado had just passed through it, with clothes, shoes, toiletries, and half-empty suitcases everywhere. The honey-coloured wooden surface of Dylan's desk was nearly hidden beneath several slippery stacks of books, notebooks, and horse magazines, while her closet stood open with uniform pieces and riding jodhpurs spilling out of it and across the room. Dylan's beloved stuffed panda, Pudding, was lying atop a pile of clean socks and underwear in the middle of the floor.

Honey's section of the room was a little neater – her stuffed bear, Woozle, was already sitting on her pillow, and the framed photo of her old pony, Rocky, was back in its place on her nightstand. But most of her clothes were still piled on her bed and her closet was empty.

The room down the hall, which Lani shared with Malory and Alexandra, looked much the same – Lani had barely bothered to shrug off her coat before bolting off with Dylan to find the rest of their friends. Catching up on gossip seemed much more important than unpacking at the moment. It was amazing how much could happen in just three weeks apart. Even though the four of them had emailed one another frequently, Lani, Dylan, Malory, and Honey still had a million things to discuss.

"So, Honey," Lani said, deciding to take pity on Malory and change the subject, "how's Sam?"

Honey's real first name was Felicity, but "Honey"

suited her perfectly, with her shoulder-length blonde hair and sweet personality.

"He's doing really well," she replied in her soft voice with its crisp British accent. "He finished his latest course of chemo just before Christmas and he's feeling much better already." She held up her hand, displaying crossed fingers. "We're trying not to get too excited yet, but the doctors are starting to use the *R*-word."

Dylan wrinkled her nose in confusion. "The *R*-word?"

"Remission?" Lani mentally thanked her sister Guadeloupe for her obsession with *General Hospital*. Random medical knowledge could come in handy. "That's awesome!" She smiled, remembering how cool Sam had been when she'd visited him with Honey. She'd quickly recognized Honey's twin as a kindred spirit – kind and sweet just like Honey, but with a decidedly devilish twist. "When you talk to him, tell him I said hi."

"I will," Honey promised. "But you could email him if you want, too. Now that he's on the mend, I know he'd – oops! What was that?"

She'd just shifted her feet and kicked something hidden in a pile of clothes, sending it skittering across the floor.

"My new iPod!" Dylan exclaimed, pouncing on the item and holding it up triumphantly. "I was afraid I'd managed to lose it already."

"Christmas present?" Lani guessed. "Guess all your shameless hint-dropping paid off, huh?"

Dylan nodded as she punched a button on the MP3 player's smooth white surface. The tiny colour screen lit up. "Check it out," she said. "Mom and Dad really came through. Not only does it hold all my tunes, but I can load my digital photos and carry them around, too. See?"

"Yeah, my sister Dacil has one of those." Lani leaned closer to get a better look at the picture that had just popped up on the screen. Her eyes widened as she took in a tall, good-looking, dark-haired guy grinning in front of a picturesque ski lodge. "Whoa! Who's that cute guy?"

"Cute guy? Where?" Malory jumped to her feet and hurried over, with Honey right behind her.

Dylan shrugged. "Oh, that's just Henri," she said, her voice sounding a little *too* casual. "I met him in Aspen when my family went skiing the week after Christmas. I'm sure I must have mentioned him..."

"No, you didn't!" Lani howled. She couldn't believe Dylan had managed to hold out on them for so long. "Henri? Does that mean he's, like, *French*?"

"He does look kind of French," Malory commented, leaning over for a better view.

Honey wrinkled her nose. "What do you mean, 'he looks kind of French'? It's not like he's wearing a beret or holding a baguette or something."

"I don't know." Malory sounded sheepish yet defiant. "He just does."

"Spill it, Walsh. Who is he?" Lani demanded, grabbing the iPod out of her friend's hands and scrolling through the next few photos. The same cute guy was featured in each of them – standing in front of a snowbank, sipping from a steaming mug in a cosy-looking lodge, even posing with his arm casually slung around Dylan's shoulders as they stood in front of a ski lift.

"He looks older than us," Honey said, peering at the photos over Lani's shoulder.

"He is." Dylan was still trying to maintain her casual demeanor but failing completely. "He's fifteen, and he's awesome! Not to mention a totally amazing skier..."

"'Dylan and Henri, sittin' in a..." Lani sang. Then she glanced at Honey. "What's the French word for tree?"

"Un arbre," Honey supplied.

"'Sittin' in *un arbre*,'?" Lani finished, rolling the *r*'s for extra emphasis.

Dylan rolled her eyes and snatched back her iPod. "Nice accent, Frenchie," she said. "Anyway, you guys can sing all the songs you want – I'm not ashamed to admit I was totally crushing on Henri the whole week." She grinned. "And who can blame me – just look at him!"

"So when's the wedding?" Malory teased.

"Not sure yet," Dylan replied easily. "Why don't you hold the first weekend in June, say, ten years from now?"

Lani laughed. That was just one of the things she loved about Dylan – she had a great sense of humour about herself. "So, are you guys going to keep in touch?" she asked.

"Sure." Dylan shrugged. "We traded email info and

stuff. But at the moment, I'm much more interested in talking about another very cute guy, though not for myself… Namely, a certain Saint Kits eighth-grader named Josh." She stared meaningfully at Honey.

Honey jumped to her feet, her cheeks flushing pink. "Come on, you lot," she said. "What are we doing sitting around here when we haven't been down to see the ponies yet?"

Lani grinned. For weeks, Dylan had been trying to convince Honey that Caleb's friend Josh could be the boy of her dreaMs It looked like Honey wasn't in the mood to discuss her social life just now. Still, even though she didn't want to let Honey get away with changing the subject, Lani had to admit she had a point about visiting the stable.

"Yeah, let's go." She headed for the door. "We can grill Honey about Josh on the way to the barn."

"Cool," Dylan agreed, kicking off the shoes she was wearing and grabbing a pair of black Ariat paddock boots, the toes of which were poking out from beneath an enormous pile of clothes. "Let me pull on my boots, though. I spent the entire break begging for these ruby flats, and my parents will kill me if I come home with them covered in manure stains."

Lani loitered in the doorway as she waited for her friends to pull on jackets and shoes for the walk down to the stable. She jumped when she heard someone clearing her throat in the hallway directly behind her. She moved aside just as a tall, blonde girl swept into the room. The newcomer stopped short, her grey-blue eyes narrowing as she took in the chaotic scene.

"That's funny," the blonde girl said coolly. "When I left this room half an hour ago, there weren't nearly so many people crammed into it."

"Nice to see you again, too, Lynsey," Lani said cheerfully. Lynsey Harrison, Dylan and Honey's third roommate, tended to enter every room as if she were a long-lost queen returning to her kingdom. Though it didn't usually bother Lani, she knew that Lynsey's attitude rubbed some people the wrong way – particularly Dylan, who'd had more than one run-in with Lynsey and her best friend, Patience, since the start of the school year.

The other three girls chorused their hellos. Honey took a step closer. "Lynsey, what did you do to your hair?" she asked. "It looks really nice!"

Lynsey looked pleased as she touched a hand to her sleek blonde tresses. "Thanks. I guess you have a good eye, Honey. Mother took me to the salon at Bergdorf's, and John Barrett did my cut and oversaw the colouring. You could call it a reward for a job well done – Mother and Daddy were totally impressed by my report card, not to mention making both the junior jumping and the field hockey team in my first year."

Dylan rolled her eyes, obviously unimpressed by Lynsey's bragging. "They say blondes have more fun," she said. "So now that you're blonder than ever, does that mean your life is a nonstop party?"

Lynsey shrugged as she flicked an imaginary speck of lint off her jeans. "I suppose so," she said. "In any case,

I'm sure it's nothing like being a redhead. Red's such a difficult colour – clashes with almost everything, doesn't it?" She glanced up at Dylan and pursed her lips. "Take what you're wearing as Exhibit A."

Dylan's smile faded fast as she glanced down at her pink Heatherette hoodie and faded 501s. "OK, listen—" she began hotly.

"Hey, Lynsey," Honey broke in, with a desperate glance at Lani to show she was trying to head off a fight on their first afternoon back. "Where'd you get those jeans? They're new, right?"

"They were a Christmas present," Lynsey conceded. She stepped farther into the room and tossed her embroidered handbag onto her bed. "They're Juicy Couture."

Lani had to admit that the jeans were cute, even though she wasn't as interested in fashion as Dylan and Lynsey. "Come on," she said. "I thought we were going down to the stable." She glanced at Lynsey. "Uh, want to come?"

"No thanks." Lynsey was sitting on her bed digging through her handbag. "I already checked on Bluegrass, and he's fine. I guess they got some decent help to take care of the horses during the break."

Lani tilted her head, trying to figure out if Lynsey's comment was supposed to be some kind of slam on the riding director, Ali Carmichael, or the regular stable help, or if it was just one of her usual careless remarks. Deciding it wasn't worth the effort to work out either way, she headed out the door into the hallway, which was crowded with other returning students.

"If you guys aren't coming now, I'm going without you!" she sang out. "Then the ponies will know who really loves them!"

Her three friends caught up by the time she'd gone ten metres. "Gee, during the break I'd almost forgotten how pleasant it is being around Lynsey," Dylan muttered. "I think I'm already breaking out in a rash."

"Forget her," Malory commanded. "We have much more important things to think about. Like how much the ponies missed us!"

Honey glanced past Lani at Malory. "So you didn't get to come check on them at all over Christmas?" she asked.

Lani had been wondering about that, too. Malory lived in Cheney Falls, the small town just a couple of miles from campus. While the rest of them had been miles away from the Chestnut Hill stable, she had been practically right next door.

"The holidays are the busiest time in Dad's shop," Malory explained. "I spent most of my spare time helping him out. I barely had time to get away for the occasional horse fix at my local barn."

"You mean the same local barn where a certain very cute guy hangs out?" Dylan inquired. "Poor Tybalt – I wonder if he knows he's only number two in your heart, Mal?"

"Very funny." Malory rolled her eyes, and Lani grinned, noticing that her friend's cheeks had gone pink. "Anyway, I did call Ms Carmichael a few times over the break to make sure Tybalt was doing OK," Malory went on. "She invited me to come over and help exercise the ponies at the end of last week, but I just couldn't do it – there were too many people crowding into the shop to exchange the shoes they got for Christmas." She shrugged. "Good for Dad's business, but not so good for my riding, I guess."

"Bad luck," Lani sympathized. "But we're here now, right? We can make up for it with tons of riding this term." She was happy to see that Malory seemed more comfortable talking about her home life these days. When the girls had first started at Chestnut Hill, Malory had kept pretty quiet about her personal situation. It had been several weeks before her friends had found out that Malory was at Chestnut Hill on a full riding scholarship, and that her recently widowed father, unlike most Chestnut Hill parents, was anything but wealthy.

"Hey, guys!" a new voice called, breaking into Lani's thoughts.

Turning, she saw Razina Jackson and Wei Lin Chang, two of their dorm mates, emerging from the stairwell and hurrying toward them. "Welcome back, you two!" Lani greeted them. "How was Tanzania, Razina?"

"Awesome, thanks." Razina smiled. Her mother owned an art gallery in New York that specialized in African pieces, and Razina often got to accompany her on sourcing trips. "We stopped off to ski the Alps on the way home, too, as usual. So did you guys go anywhere?"

"I hit the slopes, too – Aspen," Dylan told her. "It was totally fantastic. And I'm *not* just talking about the skiing."

"Oh?" Wei Lin raised her eyebrows, a curious look on her pretty, delicate face. "Do tell!"

"Well, if you insist..." Dylan began with a grin.

They spent the next few minutes trading holiday stories. Then Razina and Wei Lin spotted someone else they wanted to talk to, and Lani and her friends continued on their way. They clattered down the narrow stairwell leading to the first-floor landing, then continued down one side of the sweeping, double main staircase leading down into the lobby. Lani took the crimson-carpeted steps two at a time, eager to get to the stable as quickly as possible to see Colorado.

As they neared the foot of the steps, the noise from the lobby grew louder. The area was packed with students, parents, and staff. Some girls were just arriving back after the break, while others were showing their families around the dorm or catching up with friends and roommates. The dorm prefect, senior Noel Cousins, was replacing several ornaments that had been knocked off the dorm's elegantly decorated Christmas tree, while nearby, an unrecognizable person staggered across the crowded room, completely hidden beneath a huge pile of sports equipment.

"Well, looks like everything around here is back to normal," Malory joked, pausing on the bottom step.

"Yeah," Dylan snorted. "Including Lynsey. Could you believe the way she was bragging about her stupid haircut? Not to mention her report card – the way she was talking, you'd think she was the only person ever to get good grades at this school!"

Honey laughed. "Now, now, Dylan," she teased. "Are you sure you're not just extra sensitive about this topic for some reason?"

"Maybe a little," Dylan admitted with a rueful smile. "At least my dad was impressed by my A in history. I didn't tell him that was only because Mrs Von B is such an awesome teacher even Morello could pass her class if he tried."

Lani grinned at the image of the feisty paint pony sitting in Mrs Von Beyer's classroom, hooves and hocks crammed beneath one of the old-fashioned wooden desks. "I don't know," she joked. "That Morello is quite clever. I think he'd do better than just pass the class."

"True," Dylan agreed, leading the way across the crowded lobby. "In that case maybe I should have him sit in for me in French class."

Malory shot her a sympathetic look. "I take it French was not a shining moment on your report card."

"Don't ask." Dylan let out a groan. "That stupid language just isn't my thing. I wish I could take Spanish instead."

"Really?" Lani remarked innocently. "But what about Henri?"

Dylan's expression brightened. "He did say my accent was *très bon*." She sighed. "If only he were teaching our class instead of Mme. Dubois... But enough about me. Give me some good news. How did you guys do?" She glanced expectantly at the others.

"I did fine," Honey said. "Even in French," she added mischievously.

"No fair," Dylan retorted. "You studied it for years back in England!"

Malory laughed. "I only got a B in French, but my dad was so happy about my A-minus in maths that he threatened to put me in charge of the accounts at the shoe store." She raised her eyebrows at Lani. "Of course, I'm sure Ms Maths-and-Science here probably put us all to shame."

Lani swallowed hard. Normally she hated talking about marks because she got straight A's and didn't want to sound like she was bragging. Now that she was dealing with a less-than-perfect report card, she felt even weirder about discussing it – after all, the marks she thought were so disappointing might seem perfectly adequate to her friends. The last thing she wanted to do was make them feel bad by complaining about a handful of B's.

"Are we going to stand around here all day talking about boring school stuff, or are we going to see the horses?" she demanded, deciding the best thing was to change the subject. She reached for the lobby door, letting in a blast of cold air as she swung it open. "Come on – last one to the stable gets thrown in the muck heap!"

Chapter Three

"Hey, buddy. Remember me?" Lani opened her fingers to reveal a chunk of carrot on her palm.

The buckskin pony – whose coat was unusually dark, like a polished grey-brown pebble – reached over the half-door of his stall to grab it. He crunched the carrot quickly, then nosed at Lani with his black-tipped ears pricked forward, looking for more treats. Lani smiled and rubbed his face.

"Are you happy to see me or just my carrots?" she teased.

Dylan appeared beside her. "How's Colorado?"

"Gorgeous as always," Lani answered, tugging gently at the pony's dark forelock. "How's Morello?"

"He's fine now that I'm back," Dylan reported. "He told me he practically wasted away over the break, he was pining for me so."

Lani grinned. "Good thing you speak horse," she quipped, looking across the aisle to where a cute bay-and-white pinto face was peering out at them. "Otherwise poor Morello would be completely misunderstood."

She wandered over to the stall next door. The bottom half of the Dutch door stood ajar, and Malory was inside standing beside a lightly built dark bay pony, stroking his neck. The pony lifted his head and pointed his delicate ears forward when Lani approached, his nostrils flaring, but at a soft word from Malory he relaxed.

"Looks like Tybalt's glad to see you," Lani commented, keeping her voice soft and calm. Tybalt was still new to Chestnut Hill. He was more highly-strung than most of the other school ponies and could be spooky and unpredictable. However, he'd relaxed a great deal since Malory had been working with him, using T-touch and other natural horsemanship techniques she'd learned from the well-known horsewoman Amy Fleming. Amy practised these special healing methods on her farm, Heartland, and had taken a break from her veterinary studies at Virginia Tech to help Malory with Tybalt the previous term.

Malory looked up at her. "He seems fine." She sounded pleasantly surprised. "I was afraid he might stress out over the break with the change in routine and everything. But it looks like he took it in stride."

Dylan had followed Lani to Tybalt's stall. "Where's Honey?" she asked.

"I'm sure she's with Minuet," Malory replied, nodding at the next stall down on the other side of the aisle.

The three friends walked over to look into the stall.

They found Honey with her arms wrapped around the neck of a gorgeous grey Connemara mare. The pony, whose full name was Moonlight Minuet, was nuzzling Honey gently on the shoulder. Honey had fallen for the pretty grey pony as soon as she'd stepped out of the trailer, but all of the girls were fond of her. While Tybalt could be wary with people he didn't know, and Colorado and Morello were most enthusiastic when there were treats involved, Minnie seemed to genuinely enjoy human company. She was one of the most affectionate horses Lani had ever encountered, and her sweet temperament was a perfect match for Honey's gentle nature.

It's too bad Patience still owns her – at least technically, Lani thought as she watched Honey work a stray piece of straw out of the pony's silky mane.

Towards the end of the autumn term, Lynsey's best friend, Patience Duvall, had received the beautiful grey pony as a gift from her father. However, Patience was only a novice rider at best, and showed little interest in improving her skills. Lani and her friends suspected that if it weren't for Lynsey's ambitions on her behalf, Patience would probably drop out of riding altogether. But -whatever her idol Lynsey did, Patience wanted to do, too. And so they were all stuck with her.

The situation with Minnie had become complicated, however. When the pony had strained her tendons due to Lynsey's overzealous training, it had been Honey who nursed her back to health. Patience's father then decided to free-lease Minnie to Chestnut

Hill as a school pony until Patience was ready to take on all the responsibilities of taking care of a pony herself. Minnie still had a few more weeks of rest before she'd be ready to be used in lessons, and Lani knew that Honey, for one, was counting the days until she could have her first ride.

Dylan leaned her arms on the top edge of the Dutch door. "I'm sure Aunt Ali will let you ride Minnie in class this term once she's all better," she said. "It's totally obvious you two click!"

Honey's eyes were shining when she looked up at her friends. "Oh, I hope so!" she said, scratching Minnie's poll. "But even if she doesn't, I'm just so happy that Minnie gets to stay here."

"That's our Honey," Lani said fondly. "Always looking on the bright side!" She wasn't sure she could be so selfless herself. If the unthinkable happened and somebody like Patience were to buy Colorado, Lani wasn't sure she'd be able to stand not riding him.

I'd probably wind up sneaking down here at midnight to take him for a ride, she thought, shuddering at the thought of having her favourite pony in the world taken away from her. *On second thought, maybe not. We all know how well that sort of thing usually works out...*

Her gaze shifted to Dylan. Early last term on a dare from Lynsey, Dylan had done just that. Dylan had attempted to jump Morello over a course of fences in the dark, well after curfew. Patience had reported her to their housemother, and ever since, it had been a battle between the two of them. Dylan never passed up the chance to make a jab at Patience, and Patience had shown little love for Dylan and her friends.

After spending a few minutes saying hello to the other ponies, the four girls left the barn and headed across the stable yard to the U-shaped shed row where the faculty's personal horses were boarded. The large box stall at one end had been converted into an office for Ms Carmichael and the other riding faculty.

The office door was standing open, letting in the brisk winter air. Inside, the girls found Ali Carmichael dressed in fleece gloves and a Carhartt jacket, sitting at the large wooden desk, her head bent over an assortment of papers.

"Hi, Aunt Al – uh, I mean, Ms Carmichael," Dylan corrected herself quickly.

Lani shot her an amused look. It couldn't be easy for the Dylan to remember to address her aunt appropriately all the time. Noticing the sketches on the papers on the desk, she stepped forward for a closer look.

"Hey, what's that?" she asked. "Is it the plan for the new cross-country course?" At the end of last term, Ms Carmichael had mentioned that Chestnut Hill would be adding a cross-country course to its equestrian facilities. Lani couldn't wait – she and Colorado made a pretty good team in the show-jumping ring, but she suspected that cross-country jumping would suit them even better. They both were bold and quick-thinking, with a love of wide-open spaces and a need for speed.

Ms Carmichael's blue eyes twinkled. "Good guess, Lani," she said. "Take a look if you want. These new drawings came in this morning – I've been so busy that I've barely had a moment to take a look until now."

The girls crowded around the desk, peering at the blueprints. Lani felt a surge of excitement as her eyes jumped from one drawing to the next. Because of her father's military career, her family had moved around a lot, and Lani had been to a few three-day events in different parts of the country – one was the only four-star event in North America, the Rolex Kentucky Three-Day Event, which was held every spring at the beautiful Kentucky Horse Park in Lexington. Watching those magnificent, athletic horses galloping across the rolling terrain and hurling themselves enthusiastically over enormous, solid fences was like nothing else she'd ever seen. Combined with the precision and elegance of dressage and the technique of show-jumping, the other two phases in the sport of eventing, it was a true test of a horse and rider's athleticism and partnership. Lani couldn't wait to try it with Colorado!

"So when will the course be ready?" she prompted.

Ms Carmichael ran her fingers through her short dark hair. "Don't start tacking up yet," she warned. "Construction won't begin until things thaw out – probably after Spring Break. With any luck, the course may be finished by summer."

"Oh." Lani was a little disappointed that she wouldn't get to live out her eventing dreams any time soon. Still, she comforted herself with the thought that she still had five more years at Chestnut Hill to enjoy the cross—country course once it was ready.

Meanwhile Honey was squinting at the plans. "Is that a trakehner?" she queried, pointing to one of the sketches.

"Huh?" Dylan said, looking where Honey was pointing. "I thought Trakehner was a breed of horse."

"It is," Ms Carmichael said with a smile. "It's also a type of cross-country fence – a ditch with a rail or log over it. And yes, Honey, that's exactly what it is."

"They can be pretty scary to jump," Honey said with a shiver. Lani recalled Honey had done some low-level eventing back in England on her old pony. "They never bothered Rocky a bit," Honey went on, "but it gave me the creeps just seeing that big ditch under the jump."

"A ditch, huh? I'm sure Colorado and I can handle it," Lani said confidently. "Ditches are just about the only thing to jump out on the trail back home."

"Yeah, but remember, cowgirl," Dylan teased, "you won't have the horn of that big Western saddle to hang on to out on the cross-country course."

Lani grinned. Dylan and others at Chestnut Hill liked to tease her gently about her Western riding experience. In Colorado Springs and several of the other places she'd lived out west, it could be challenging to find an English stable where she could take hunter-jumper lessons. Instead, she had ridden wherever she could, and along the way had learned about several different Western sports, from reining to cutting and barrel racing. She'd also done lots of trail riding through the rugged terrain and spectacular scenery of the Rocky Mountains.

"Keep in mind, girls, that proper cross-country riding isn't just running and jumping willy-nilly," Ms Carmichael cautioned. "The most important thing is to stay safe. That's why eventers are required to wear helmets and safety vests for the cross-country phase of a competition, and it's also why we're going to spend time this term preparing ourselves and the horses so we'll be ready to go when the fences are in place."

"Cool," Dylan said. "So what are we going to do first?"

"Well, a lot of what we already do in class is good training." Ms Carmichael leaned back in her chair and rested one booted foot on her other knee. "For instance, dressage builds up basic muscle strength and improves our communication and partnership with the horses, while jumping through different gymnastics helps the horse work out how to problem-solve on course. That's important in case you need to count on him to get you both out of trouble."

"Sounds like this term is going to be all about eventing!" Lani quipped.

Ms Carmichael smiled. "Not quite," she said. "But we will be having a nutrition symposium headed up by a member of the US Equestrian Team. So you might get some cross-country tips then."

"See?" Lani grinned at her friends. "All about eventing!" She couldn't wait to tackle something new with Colorado.

* * *

For the next few days, Lani was too busy to spend much time daydreaming about cross-country riding or anything else. She was already doing her best to stick to her vow to keep up with her schoolwork, which meant spending more time than she would have liked doing maths problems and reading endless chapters on the Revolutionary War and the Constitutional Convention. She'd also volunteered to take on several extra-credit projects – an optional science project, a bonus English essay, even a challenging French translation project – hoping to get her marks back on track as quickly as possible. On top of that, her first few riding classes of the term reminded her that she'd let her muscles get out of shape over the past three weeks.

Almost before she knew it, Friday had arrived and she was walking out of French, her last class of the day.

"TGIF!" Dylan moaned as the four friends fell into step and headed outside. "I thought the weekend would never get here."

Malory glanced at her in genuine surprise as she zipped up her parka. "Really? I thought this first week totally flew by."

"You wouldn't say that if Mme. Dubois thought *you* were the worst thing to happen to the French language since Pépé Le Pew." Dylan pulled a blue knit hat out of her coat pocket and yanked it on over her red hair. "And by the way, brrr!" she complained. "Is it spring yet?"

Lani laughed. "If you think *this* is cold, you'd better

not visit me in Colorado," she teased. "It gets colder than this in May sometimes."

"I repeat: brrr!" Dylan said, fishing a pair of matching blue gloves out of her pocket. "And might I remind you, I just got back from Colorado – Aspen, home of gorgeous French guys, remember?"

"Oui, oui!" Lani replied. "I guess you didn't notice the cold when you were gazing into Henri's big brown eyes, huh?"

"Exactly." Dylan finished pulling on her gloves and hunched her shoulders against the wind.

The four girls started across the broad, flat lawn that lay between the academic buildings and the student centre, their shoes crunching on the wintry grass. As they walked, Lani noticed that Honey had lagged behind, pulling out the new BlackBerry her parents had given her for Christmas to help her keep up with news about her brother.

"Hey, any messages from Sam?" she asked, slowing her step to match Honey's.

Honey looked up quickly, her cheeks turning pink. She tucked the BlackBerry back in her bag and started playing with the edge of her grey uniform blazer, which was poking out from beneath her winter coat. "Oh! Um, yeah – he wrote yesterday. He's doing well."

"Cool." Lani narrowed her eyes and studied her friend's heart-shaped face. "But that's not a 'my brother is recovering' face. That's a 'there's something I'm not telling my friends' face."

By now Dylan and Malory had stopped and were

staring at Honey, too. "You're right, Lani," Dylan declared. "She does look suspicious." Putting her hands on her hips, she did her best to look stern. "Now, are you going to tell us why, Honey? Or do we have to tickle it out of you?" She wriggled her fingers threateningly.

Honey backed up and held up both hands, laughing. "No tickling. Oh, please, no tickling – I give up!" Honey gasped for air between her laughter. "It's not that big a deal, really," she said, composing herself.

"We'll be the judges of that." Lani crossed her arms over her chest. "Now spill it."

"I just got an email from Josh," Honey confessed. "You know – Caleb's friend at Saint Kits?"

Dylan clutched her head and gasped. "What? How could you even think about keeping this kind of news from us? I'm hurt! I'm insulted! I'm totally offended!"

Malory poked her in the arm. "Shush," she ordered. "Let her tell us."

"It's nothing much, really," Honey protested. "He was just asking if I'm going into Cheney Falls tomorrow."

"Whoa, that sounds suspiciously like he's asking you out on a date!" Lani exclaimed. She and Dylan had been plotting to get Honey together with Caleb's cute friend for ages – could it finally be happening? "But surely you wouldn't say that a date is not that big a deal?"

"Wait," Malory said. "You can't go into town tomorrow, Honey. Remember? We're having a make-up riding class since we missed out on Monday."

"Oh. True." Honey looked a little disappointed. "So much for that."

"What do you mean, so much for that?" Dylan rolled her eyes. "It's not such a bad thing playing hard to get, you know. Just email him back and tell him you *might* go next week instead."

Honey looked dubious. "But didn't Ms Carmichael say we might have an optional class next Saturday, too, because the equine dentist is coming next week?"

"Of course." Dylan sighed loudly and rolled her eyes. "But you don't have to tell *Josh* that, silly! Let him wait and wonder!"

Honey still didn't look convinced. "Maybe I'll see if he'll be there two weeks from tomorrow," she said. "We'll probably go into town then, right?"

Dylan grinned. "I think that's long enough to make him wait!"

They were passing the modern, glass-and-cedar, octagonal-shaped library building by then. The bright winter sun was low in the sky, reflecting off the tall windows, which made Lani squint as she glanced ahead toward Adams House.

"Come on," she said, picking up her pace a little. "If we hurry up and change clothes, we can fit in a quick visit to the stable before dinner. I told Ms Carmichael I'd pull Colorado's mane – he's looking like shaggy."

She was looking forward to her first weekend back at Chestnut Hill. After all the extra work she was already doing for her classes, she figured she deserved a break.

She was still smiling at that thought when she and her friends entered the dorm. The lobby was deserted except for their assistant housemother, a tall, slim young woman named Jacqueline Sebastian, who was standing by the table in the middle of the lobby flipping through a stack of envelopes. She looked up when she heard them enter.

"Lani Hernandez," she said. "Just the person I was looking for. There's a letter for you."

"For me? Thanks." Lani hurried forward to take the envelope from Jacqueline. Snail mail was a rare event, usually consisting of the occasional care package or birthday card from her grandparents or other older relatives.

Dylan peered over her shoulder. "Who's it from?"

"My parents," Lani said, looking at the return address, written in her father's distinctive spiky handwriting. "I wonder why they're writing to me."

She slit open the envelope with her fingernail and pulled out the single sheet of paper inside. It was covered in her father's writing, and she scanned it quickly.

Dear Lani,

I hope your first week back at school is going well.

I'm sure you're surprised to get a letter from me. I thought about calling you to discuss this, but I felt that I needed to get everything down on paper so you can see exactly where your mother and I are coming from, and somehow this seemed too important for email.

The thing is, your mother and I have been discussing you a lot these past few weeks. Perhaps we should have talked to you over the holidays. But we weren't sure what to say, and things being so hectic with all the comings and goings, we let it slide. But now that things have calmed down again, it's time to let you know what's on our minds.

I must admit, Lani, your last report card caught us by surprise. I guess we just take it for granted that all our girls will bring home top marks. We've always been proud of that – not only does it show off those sharp Hernandez brains, but more important, it means you're working to your potential and setting yourselves up for a bright future.

We know you're enjoying yourself at Chestnut Hill, *but we fear that perhaps you're enjoying yourself a little too much for your own good. It's wonderful that you've made friends and that your riding is progressing so well. But those things seem to be making your marks suffer, and we're very concerned. The most important thing we can give you, aside from our love and support, is a top-notch education that will set you up for a good, happy life down the road.*

If Chestnut Hill *isn't a place where you can get that, we need to talk about other options. For instance, there's your sisters' school in* California *– it doesn't have horseback riding, but it has a terrific sports programme that would allow you to continue playing softball while still getting that top education. You would also have your sisters there to help you settle in.*

Your mother will be flying in to meet me in DC *next weekend, and we've made an appointment to meet with*

Dr Starling the Wednesday after next at 4 p.m. We'd like you to attend this meeting as well, so you can give us your perspective on all this.

No matter what happens, please understand that we're only trying to do what's best for you. As I'm so fond of saying, every new experience helps shape who we are, and that includes the time you have spent at Chestnut Hill. We just have to remember that it's never too late to change direction, however tough it seems.

Love,

Dad

Lani stared at the letter in her hand, wondering if this was a bad dream. *Her parents wanted her to leave Chestnut Hill!*

Chapter Four

"Lani, what's the matter?" Malory asked. "Is your family OK? Is someone ill?"

Lani knew it was no use trying to hide her emotions from her sensitive friend. "No!" she exclaimed. "My parents are just completely demented, that's all! They're totally freaking out because I didn't get straight A's."

"Really? What did you get?" Honey asked.

Lani shrugged sheepishly. "OK, don't kill me for keeping secrets, OK? I didn't tell you guys before because I was kind of embarrassed. But I got mostly B's – only two A's."

"Are you kidding?" Dylan stared at her. "My parents would kill for that kind of report card! Especially from Chestnut Hill!"

"Can you call and tell my parents that, please?" Lani was only half joking. "I can't believe they're making such a big fat stinking deal out of a couple of measly B's. I mean, like I said, I wasn't exactly thrilled about them, either. But you don't see me beating myself up about it!" She shook the letter, which was still clutched in her hand. "I'm going to go call my dad right now and give him a piece of my mind!"

She marched off toward the pay phones at one end of the lobby, since she didn't have a mobile. Before she got more than a few steps, she felt Dylan yanking her to a halt.

"Hold it," Dylan ordered. "This is the overreaction police, and I've got a warrant."

Lani rolled her eyes and snorted. "Very funny," she said. "Now let me go. I need to do something about this."

"Um, are you sure about that?" Malory asked diplomatically. "I mean, calling up your folks all upset and mutinous..."

"I am mutinous, and they should know it!" But Lani slumped a little, realizing her friends were right. Her father wasn't the type of person to react well to hysterical, accusatory phone calls. "So what am I supposed to do?" she demanded with a frown. "I know my parents. They're very methodical and stuff. If they went to all the trouble of writing this letter, they're serious about this." She shook her head grimly. "I should have known they wouldn't just let those marks pass. This is so like them – they were just figuring out their line of attack."

"That's a little harsh, isn't it?" Dylan said. "I mean, all parents freak out about marks and stuff. It's, like, their job. Just give them some time – they'll get over it."

Honey nodded so vigorously that her blonde hair bounced. "Especially if you bring your marks up this term, as I'm sure you will," she added. "Didn't you just volunteer for that extra-credit project in science? Let them see how well you're doing now that you're all settled in."

"But they didn't even give me a chance to defend myself before they started making threats," Lani protested. "How fair is that?"

At that moment a group of Adams upperclassmen burst into the lobby, bringing with them a torrent of chatter and laughter along with a sudden blast of cold air from outside.

"Come on, let's go upstairs," Honey suggested. "We can discuss this more over dinner, OK, Lani?"

"Sure, I guess." Lani shoved the letter into her jacket pocket and followed her friends, who were drifting toward the stairs. Now that her first burst of indignation had passed, she was starting to think more carefully about what her father had written.

He didn't come right out and say they're definitely yanking me out of Chestnut Hill, she thought. *But it's obvious that's what they're thinking. I can't believe they would do that because of one lousy report card!* She blew out a sigh of frustration. *Why do my parents have to be so intense about all this education stuff? I know they believe in working hard and making the most of your opportunities, but sometimes they go too far. Like when Dacil messed up on that maths test and Mom and Dad made her go to a tutor for the rest of the term, or the time in fifth grade when they made me write that make-up essay during our family trip to the Grand Canyonæ*

Like her older sisters, Lani had attended local state schools through the sixth grade. Also like them, she had always played a variety of sports, from track and tennis to her favorite team sport, softball, which she still played regularly at Chestnut Hill. Unlike her sisters, however, she had also become utterly fascinated with horseback riding – starting with the first year of hunt-seat lessons she'd taken at age six while the family was living in Georgia, and continuing on through the Western riding she'd done over the past few years in Colorado Springs.

So when the time came to start boarding school, Lani had decided that she didn't want to leave riding behind. Since the boarding school that Dacil and Guadeloupe attended didn't have a riding programme, she started researching schools that did. She had known Chestnut Hill was for her from the moment she'd found its website during an online search. The first thing that had caught her attention was the gorgeous action photo of a galloping horse – the dressage instructor's part-Thoroughbred gelding, Harold, she'd later found out – at the top of the page about the riding programme. But the rest of the site had impressed her, too, from the description of the academics to the list of illustrious alumni.

Her parents had been sceptical at first, but Lani's exhaustive research, carefully crafted arguments, and overwhelming enthusiasm had won them over and they'd agreed to let her go to Chestnut Hill. They had even told her how proud they were of her independence and initiative in finding it. And now that she was here, she was even more certain that it was the best school for her. Not only did it have a strong academic program, but where else could she hope to have such great riding opportunities?

And more importantly, she added to herself, clutching the stair rail tightly, *where else could I hope to make such amazing friends?*

"Lani? You coming?"

Lani glanced up and saw that her friends were already on the first-floor landing. She headed after them, taking the staircase three steps at a time to catch up.

"I hate to tell you, but I don't think you'll have time to pull Colorado's mane today," Malory said as Lani joined the others. "We only have half an hour before dinner. I heard they're serving lasagna tonight – yum! We don't want to be late for that."

"That's OK. I can do it some other time." Lani checked her watch as they all wandered toward Honey and Dylan's room. "I should probably bang out those French verb conjugations, anyway."

"Homework – on a Friday night?" Dylan put her hand over her heart and raised her eyebrows in shock. "Are you running a fever or something?"

Lani forced a smile. "Hey, the sooner I get it out of the way, the sooner I can relax and enjoy the weekend, right?"

"If you say so." Dylan shrugged. "As for me, I plan to start relaxing right away. Live for today!" Pumping her fist in the air, she dived into her room.

The others laughed and dispersed as well. Back in her own room, Lani changed out of her uniform into a pair of flannel-lined khakis and her favourite faded brown Abercrombie sweater. Then she sat down at her desk and opened her French textbook. She sat there for a long moment staring at the words on the page without really seeing them. It wasn't going to be easy to give up hanging out at the barn with her friends, or to limit her time with Colorado to riding classes alone. But that's what she'd have to do to make sure her marks improved before her parents' meeting with Dr Starling.

But it'll be worth it, she reminded herself fiercely. *Better to miss him a little bit for a couple of weeks than miss him a lot forever.*

It was only then that she suddenly realized she hadn't told her friends the part about her parents' meeting with Chestnut Hill's principal. Making a mental note to fill them in over dinner, she did her best to focus her attention on her textbook. But she'd barely finished one section of conjugations when the door burst open, and Dylan bounced in with Honey and Malory at her heels.

"Ready to go eat?" Dylan demanded. "I'm starving. Plus, I want to show off my stellar new shoes – I've barely had a chance to wear them yet." Grinning, she stuck out one foot to show off her green Fornarina sneakers, which she'd received for Christmas. Since she wasn't allowed to wear such casual shoes with her school uniform, they – along with the three other new pairs of shoes she'd acquired over the holidays – had been relegated to dinner and other after-hours activities.

"Sure." Lani stood up, pushing her textbook away. After all, her parents would hardly want her to starve for the sake of her French mark. "Let's go."

Soon the four friends were on the path leading to the student centre, where the cafeteria was located. Other students were also thronging toward the same spot, most of them huddled into their coats against the winter air, which was getting chillier now that the sun had set.

Normally the dinner hour was one of Lani's favourite times of the day. But tonight she was way too distracted by her parents' letter to look forward to a relaxing meal.

I need to do something – work out a solid plan to change Mom's and Dad's minds about Chestnut Hill, she thought. *It's the only way I'll get through the next few days – let alone the next two weeks – without freaking out. I feel like I'm about to explode.*

She smiled in spite of her worry, realizing she had just echoed one of her eldest sister, Marta's, favourite expressions. How many times had she heard Marta threaten to explode during one of her arguments with their -parents?

But she never did, Lani thought. *She always seemed to work through things and come up with some strategy. And it almost always worked…*

That gave her an idea. As she and her friends burst

into the warm student centre lobby and turned toward the cafeteria entrance, Lani put out an arm to stop the others. "Um, I'm not really that hungry," she said. "Plus, I just thought of something I need to do. Go ahead and I'll meet up with you in a little while."

"Are you sure?" Honey looked concerned. "Is something wrong?"

"Yeah," Dylan commented. "It's not like Lani Hernandez to be late for a meal," Dylan added. "Especially lasagna. You do know it has cheese in it?"

"Is it about the letter?" Malory asked.

Lani smiled, touched by her friends' concern but too distracted to stick around and explain at the moment. "Look, it's no big deal. I'll fill you in later. Save me a seat, OK?"

She scooted off before the others could say anything else, losing herself in the crowd of other students in the lobby. A few minutes later, she was entering the computer room on the second floor. This was the spot where students who didn't have BlackBerrys or laptops could go to check their email. At this hour the place was nearly deserted, with only a couple of junior girls leaning over one of the monitors giggling. That meant Lani had her choice of terminals. Picking one at the other end of the room from the upperclassmen, she sat down and logged on. Opening a new message, she entered her eldest sister's email address and then began typing furiously, her fingers flying over the computer keys.

from: ponygurllani
to: Mherndz04
subject: grrrrrrr!!!!!!
Hey Marta,
I can't believe Dad!!!!!
Did he or Mom tell u what they're doing? They're threatening 2 take me out of Chestnut Hill!!!!!! Can u believe that? Just b/c my grades weren't ultraperfect, they think I'm 2 -distracted w/horses & friends. It's like they don't want me 2 have a life! Totally not fair.

So what do u think? I'm sure D & G would luv to see me forced 2 go 2 their school. But u understand, don't u? Plz say u do... And plz tell me u have some ideas about what I should do 2 change their minds. I need a plan!

B/c if they yank me out of here, I may never b able 2 4give them...

☹☹☹☹☹☹☹☹☹

Your sis,
Lani

Without pausing to read over the email, Lani immediately hit send, tapping the mouse so hard it jumped off the pad. The computer let out a beep and flashed "Your mail has been sent" at her.

Then she logged off and sat back in her chair, already

feeling a little better. Marta would know what to do – she always did. Lani couldn't count the number of times she had gone to her eldest sister for help or advice. Marta had a knack for seeing both sides of an issue. She shared some of Lani's impulsive, idealistic attitudes toward life, but she also seemed to understand the more methodical, disciplined nature of the rest of the family in a way Lani couldn't. That was why Marta had been able to convince her parents to let her study political science instead of medicine at college without leaving them dismayed and disappointed. Lani needed a little of that Marta magic right now.

Boy do I need it, she thought as she headed out of the computer room. *Because if I don't get it...*

She banished the rest of the thought with a shudder. This was no time to panic – she had work to do if she was going to make this situation better. She walked downstairs, pausing briefly near the cafeteria entrance before continuing outside and heading back to her dorm. She wasn't going to give up – not now, not ever. But she also wasn't quite ready to act as if everything was normal again.

"Hey, what happened to you?"

Lani was lying on her bed munching her way through a bag of sour-cream-and-onion-flavoured potato crisps and trying to distract herself with the latest issue of *Practical Horseman* when Malory and their other roommate, Alexandra, returned from dinner. She glanced up at Malory's question.

"Just wasn't in the mood for lasagna after all," she said. "Sorry. I hope I didn't make you guys worry."

"I never thought I'd hear you say that," Alexandra said in surprise.

Lani couldn't help grinning. She was famous at the Chestnut Hill cafeteria for once finishing a full four servings of their famous lasagna in one sitting – beating Dylan's previous record of three and a half. "Yeah, I always said pigs would fly someday," she quipped. Before the other two could ask any more difficult questions, she nodded toward the slim box Malory was holding. "What's that?"

Malory held it up. "It's the eventing DVD Ms Carmichael is passing around," she said. "The one about the US three-day team. Paris Mackenzie and the other Curie girls just finished with it, so we get it next. We thought we'd go watch it in the common room. The others are meeting us there."

"Oh." The last thing Lani felt like doing at the moment was watching an eventing film. Why torture herself now that she knew she might never get to enjoy the feeling of flying over a cross-country course with Colorado? On the other hand, maybe watching the DVD was as good a way as any to take her mind off her probleMs She rolled to a sitting position, tossing her magazine aside. "OK, I'm in, I guess."

"Not me!" Alexandra wrinkled her nose. While she rode in the basic class and loyally cheered for her friends on the junior jumping team at their shows and other big events, she wasn't particularly interested in horse sports outside of that. "I'm going to the computer lab for a while. See you guys at lights-out."

After their roommate had left, Malory turned to face Lani. "You're acting kind of weird," she said bluntly. "Are you still worried about what your parents wrote about your marks?"

"Sort of." Lani bit her lip. Malory had a talent for reading people's feelings, and Lani wasn't very good at faking hers. Besides, she knew that if there was one time she needed her friends' help and support, it was now. "See, there was a little more in the letter than what I told you earlier."

"Really? What?"

Lani took a deep breath. "My parents think Chestnut Hill might not be the right place for me. You know, academically. They think I might be better off at my sisters' school in California."

"What?" Malory's eyes widened. "No! They can't really believe that, can they?"

Lani shrugged. "Can. Do." She tugged at a strand of her short-cropped hair. "And once they make up their minds about something like this, they totally turn into pod people. They get really focused on fixing whatever it is they think is wrong – whatever it takes." She quickly filled her friend in on everything, including the meeting with Dr Starling.

"Wow." For a moment, Malory seemed at a loss for words. "OK, but you can't just give up, right? You've got to prove they're wrong about this – study harder or something."

"Give up? *Moi?* No way!" Lani smiled, trying to muster up all her powers of optimism to chase away the anxious look on her friend's face. "I'm not giving up until they drag me out of this place kicking and screaming."

"Good." Malory looked relieved. "So what's your plan?"

"Plan?" Lani toyed with the edge of her crisp bag. "Um..."

Malory grimaced, then glanced down at the DVD in her hand. "Well, let's go to the common room. Maybe the others will have some ideas... Oh." She shot a quick, questioning glance at Lani. "If you were planning to tell them about this, I mean."

"Of course!" Lani said, climbing to her feet. "Misery loves company, right? And there's power in numbers. And four heads are better than one. And too many cooks spoil the broth. No wait! Scratch that one. There's no such thing as too many cooks when you're hungry, and in that case, broth just isn't going to cut it. Now if you're talking lasagna or sour-cream potato crisps, on the other hand—"

"OK, enough!" Malory waved her hands, laughing. "I get the idea. Now come on, let's go tell Honey and Dylan."

By the next day when the girls headed down to the stables for their Saturday riding lesson, Honey and Dylan were fully up to speed on the whole situation. Dylan spent most of the short walk from

Adams coming up with one outlandish plan after another.

"...or maybe we could pretend Lani was kidnapped," she suggested, tapping the riding crop she was carrying against the top of her suede half-chaps. "Or get her into the Witness Protection Programme."

Malory rolled her eyes. "Yeah, right," she said. "While we're at it, why don't you suggest she switch identities with Patience Duvall? That would kill two birds with one stone."

"Ooh! Awesome idea."

"Stop it, you two," Honey chided. "We've got to think of a real plan if we want to help change her parents' minds."

"Honey's right. I keep telling you guys – you just don't get it. My parents are dead serious about this. They aren't going to change their minds unless I can convince them they're wrong." Lani's voice was sharper than she'd intended. "And, I assure you, that won't be easy."

"Sorry," Malory said, shooting her a sideways glance. "We're just trying to figure out a way to keep you here with us where you belong."

As Dylan started arguing with Malory about the practicalities of the Patience/Lani identity switch, Honey dropped her voice to a whisper. "Trust me, I know exactly what it's like to have your parents make decisions that don't feel right to you, even if they have your best interests in mind," she said to Lani.

Lani knew her friend was thinking of her brother,

Sam. Until recently, Honey's parents had tried to keep the worst of his illness from her, not understanding that it only made things that much harder for her when she couldn't visit him.

"Yeah, I know," Lani muttered. Her gaze fell on the slim silver bracelet Honey was wearing, which was peeking out from under the sleeve of her riding parka. There were several charms on it, including a tiny, perfect horseshoe-shaped one Honey had told them Sam had given her for Christmas. That alone made the bracelet instantly one of Honey's most precious possessions – even with Sam in remission, Honey would never forget the horror of nearly losing her twin. Seeing the horseshoe charm, Lani felt a surge of guilt. How could she be acting like such a brat, snapping at her friends and such, when Honey had stayed her usual sweet, caring self even while facing a much more serious personal problem?

But Honey didn't seem to begrudge Lani taking centre stage. "This is awful," she declared. "We can't simply give up, can we?"

"No way!" Dylan and Malory chorused.

"You're right." Lani straightened up, regaining her flagging optimism thanks to her friends' support. "Thanks, guys."

Some of that optimism had seeped away by the time she had Colorado tacked up. The reality of her parents' intentions had soaked in overnight, and she was having trouble focusing on anything else. Every time she went through one of the familiar motions of getting him ready – picking his feet, straightening the saddle pad after he tried to shrug it off, tightening his girth one hole at a time as he preferred – she wondered exactly how many more times she would be doing it. When he turned to snuffle at her hair as she lifted the bit toward his mouth, she smiled at him, resisting the urge to plant a kiss on the end of his velvety nose.

"Hurry up," an impatient voice said from just outside the stall. Glancing out, Lani saw Lynsey standing there with her glossy blue roan pony, Bluegrass. "Aren't you ready yet? You're going to make us all late. Some of us have lives outside this stable, you know."

"Sorry," Lani murmured, although Lynsey had already moved on.

Lani quickly buckled Colorado's noseband and pulled the reins over his head. Soon she was leading him into the jumping arena, where most of the intermediate riding class was already warming up. Dylan was doing some bending exercises on Morello, while Malory guided Tybalt through a long-and-low trot warm-up meant to settle and relax him. Honey was riding a pony named Falcon that day, and she already had the dark bay gelding trotting nicely on the bit. Nadia Smith, who had been promoted from basic riding to the intermediate class at the beginning of the new term, was standing on the mounting block, grumbling under her breath and holding her dancing pony's reins with one hand as she tried to untangle her left stirrup leather from the right. Lynsey had just mounted and was leaning over to check her girth, and Paris Mackenzie and Heidi Johnson were walking and trotting at the far end of the ring.

Lani breathed deeply, taking it all in. She adjusted her stirrups, then checked her girth one last time and swung up into the saddle, bypassing the otherwise-occupied mounting block. As she settled into the well-broken-in leather seat, she found herself feeling an uncharacteristic surge of depression. Today's riding class was supposed to be focused on skills they would need for cross-country jumping. Why was she bothering to go through the motions when there was a good chance she wouldn't be around by the time the cross-country course was ready?

I can't think that way, she told herself firmly. *I have to stay positive, or I've got no chance at all. Now, buck up, cowgirl!*

But even as the lesson started, she couldn't quite shake her sense of despondency. She went through all the motions, but her heart wasn't in it. Luckily Colorado seemed to be in an agreeable mood; he could be stubborn and headstrong, often beginning a ride with his head straight up in the air and his back stiff and resistant. But for once he seemed willing to put his head down, lengthen his stride, and follow along behind the other ponies all on his own. Lani knew that even though she looked OK, she wasn't riding nearly as well as she usually did. However, she couldn't seem to make herself snap out of her glum, passive mood. She was actually glad for the chance to sit and rest about fifteen minutes into the lesson, while several of the other girls rode through the combination Ms Carmichael had set up along one fence line.

I've got to snap out of it, she told herself, nudging Colorado into a free spot by the rail. *What's wrong with me, anyway? Since when do I give up without a fight?*

She watched blankly as Lynsey and Bluegrass made a flawless trip through the gymnastic, followed by an equally strong Dylan and Morello. In Lani's mind, the cross rails and simple verticals disappeared, replaced by logs, stone walls, brush fences, and other cross-country obstacles. Lynsey and Dylan would be jumping those things within a matter of months. Would Lani be there, too? Or would she be stuck out in California, miles from anything resembling a horse?

"OK, Lani," Ms Carmichael called, breaking into her gloomy thoughts. "It's your turn. Let's see you take Colorado through. Nice and easy – trot in over the cross rail and then just let the jumps come to you."

Flustered by being caught daydreaming, Lani gathered up her reins too quickly, causing Colorado to jerk up his head in alarm. He danced to one side, his nostrils flaring and his tail swishing with annoyance.

"Sorry, boy," Lani whispered to him. Adjusting her reins, she urged him into a trot, aiming at the opening trot poles while directing her gaze at the middle of the first cross rail.

Colorado's ears pricked forward, and he lowered his head and broke into a choppy canter.

"Trot in!" Ms Carmichael called. "Trot!"

"Sorry!" Lani called breathlessly, half-halting for all she was worth. The trot poles were coming up too fast, and she ended up yanking on the right rein to turn him out at the last second.

"Yee-haw. Time for the cattle drive," Lynsey commented to Patience, just loudly enough for Lani to hear as she trotted past.

Her face flaming, Lani scowled at her. Then she took a few deep breaths, trying to calm herself so she could settle Colorado and try again. Out of the corner of her eye, she could see Malory and Dylan exchanging a surprised glance.

"It's OK," Ms Carmichael called. "Don't overthink it, Lani."

Colorado felt tense beneath her as she turned him toward the line of obstacles once again. But Lani didn't dare stop or pull out again.

Cowgirl up, Hernandez, she told herself. *You can do this.*

She half-halted strongly a few strides out, not wanting Colorado to think about breaking to a canter again before they got there. This time the pony stayed in trot, but his head was up and the gait felt rushed and strung out. Lani kept posting rather than going into two-point over the poles as the others had done, hoping the rhythm would help him settle. But he seemed to be paying no attention to her at all. One front hoof struck the first trot pole as he rushed over it, and each stride after that felt a bit off. When he reached the cross rail, he didn't bother to jump, merely lifting his feet a little higher and trotting over it. One of his hind feet connected with the wooden pole with a heavy *clunk*.

Lani winced on his behalf, then froze as she saw the next element – a small vertical – coming up. *We're supposed to be cantering now,* she thought frantically, remembering how smoothly Bluegrass and Morello had swept through the exercise just moments ago.

There was no time to fit in the canter stride, so Lani just kicked on and hoped for the best. Colorado lurched over the vertical from a rapid trot, landing at a canter this time and lunging forward.

"Easy, boy," Lani hissed, sitting back and half-halting, trying to reel in his stride.

But the feisty buckskin had had enough of her distracted, tentative riding for one day. Ignoring her aids, he launched himself at the second vertical, completely leaving out the next canter stride.

"Whoa!" Lani shouted as she felt herself left behind. Her seat thumped down on the saddle and she grabbed at a hunk of black mane to avoid catching Colorado in the mouth. She heard the top rail of the jump clatter to the ground behind them as her pony's hind legs caught it. Colorado let out a small buck before taking off at a gallop.

It took three circles to bring him down, and by the time she trotted back to the group and stopped at the end of the line next to Honey, Lani was feeling like the world's worst rider. The entire class was staring at her.

Even Lynsey appeared to be speechless for once.

"Well," Ms Carmichael said with a sympathetic smile. "That could have gone more smoothly, couldn't it? You OK, Lani?"

"Sure," Lani said, not sure whether to laugh or cry after that performance. Normally she was more the laughing type, but at the moment she was afraid she might be a little too close to tears. "And don't worry – I'm prepared to go back to the beginner class," she added. "Maybe learning how to trot over single poles on the ground would do me some good."

Ms Carmichael chuckled. "I don't think that'll be necessary," she said. She glanced at the others. "Although I suspect everyone can see now why I keep pestering you all to rely on power rather than speed to get through this sort of combination." She turned back to Lani and winked. "Ms Hernandez here just gave a perfect demonstration of what happens when you forget that."

"Glad to be of service," Lani said with a ghost of her usual humour.

The other girls laughed, and Ms Carmichael rolled her eyes. "All right," she said. "Seriously, Lani, I know you and Colorado are capable of much better than what we just saw. Give me a moment to reset the jumps, and you can give it another try."

What's the point? Lani thought, letting her reins go slack and slumping in the saddle. *Why bother to work on getting Colorado ready for that cross-country course when I'm not going to be here to ride it with him?*

"I don't think I want to go again," she called as the instructor turned away.

Ms Carmichael turned back, looking surprised. "What? Why not?"

Lani blew out a frustrated sigh. "I just don't see the point if I—" She stopped as Honey drew in a sharp breath beside her. Glancing over, Lani saw Honey shaking her head warningly.

Lani frowned, realizing that her friend had guessed what she was about to blurt out – and that she was right to warn against it. Ms Carmichael didn't know Lani was completely consumed by the possibility that she might be forced to leave Chestnut Hill. It wouldn't be fair to take it out on her – or Colorado. He deserved to go through the gymnastic with a rider who was paying attention.

"Never mind," she said lamely. "I – I just meant maybe I should trot him around first to settle him. Is that OK?"

Ms Carmichael shrugged. "Sure, take him around once or twice while I'm resetting the jumps," she said. "Then be ready to try it again, please. And just try to relax and remember what we talked about this time."

Lani nodded, then gathered up her reins. Giving the pony a cluck and a firm nudge with her legs, she headed for the rail.

I may or may not be leaving at the end of the term, she told herself. *But either way I'm here now, so I might as well follow Dylan's motto and live for today.*

Chapter Five

from: Mherndz04
to: ponygurllani
subject: re: grrrrrrr!!!!!!

Dear Lani,

Sorry I didn't get back to u sooner; just got home from a marathon cram session (yes, already! My profs are trying to kill me!).

I can tell you're upset about this. I don't blame you.

But think on this, lil sis: Daddy admires persistence. That's why he let you go to CH in the first place, remember? B/c you worked hard, did your research, and proved to him that it was a good idea.

So now you have to figure out how to prove that you still belong there. You need to show him you can balance everything: riding, softball, friends, and, most important, your academics. If you can take responsibility and show him that you're getting back on track, he'll notice. He's not an ogre, just a caring father who wants the best for us. So show him CH is the best for you, and you're golden!

Love,
Marta

Lani stared moodily at the computer screen. After riding class, she had gone straight to the student centre to check her email before it was time to get ready for dinner.

It's easy for Marta to say I need to buckle down and prove I can do it all, she thought with a scowl, playing absently with the zipper on her chaps. *She's super-smart – it's always been easy for her to keep up with schoolwork even when she's playing sports and stuff.*

Lani was smart, too, but she was also realistic enough to know she didn't share Marta's impressive powers of focus and organization. Still, she had to admit that her sister was right. Proving she could do whatever it took to excel at Chestnut Hill did seem like the only way to change her father's mind.

"Hey, so this is where you ran off to!"

Startled, Lani turned to find Dylan hurrying toward her. "Oh, hey," she greeted her. "What are you doing here?"

"You disappeared so fast after riding class that we sent out a search party." Dylan grinned. "No, just kidding. I came to email Henri – it's way easier to type on these computers than on my BlackBerry." She gazed curiously at Lani. "We *were* wondering where you went, though. You acted kind of weird after riding class."

Lani smiled. "Don't worry, I haven't been taken over by the pod people," she said. "I'm just kind of distracted. You know – this whole thing with my marks. I guess it got to me a little during class today."

"I hear you." Dylan plopped down on the seat beside her. "Did your sister write back?"

Lani had told her friends about her impulsive email the night before. "Uh-huh. She thinks I should just buckle down and prove I can do it all and still keep my marks up." She shrugged. "If only it were that easy."

"Maybe it is." Dylan leaned forward. "It's got to be worth a try, isn't it?"

"What do you mean?"

"Set yourself some goals," Dylan urged. "Make sure you ace that history test next week, and get an A on your English paper, and keep up with all Mme. D's ridiculous French assignments. Prove to your parents that you can balance work and play right here at Chestnut Hill, and they'll drop this crazy plan to ship you off somewhere else. Maybe they'll even cancel that stupid meeting next week."

Lani squeezed her eyes shut, hating those words: *that stupid meeting next week*. "OK. I'm with you. But how am I supposed to convince them of all that by next Wednesday?"

"I don't know," Dylan admitted. "But all you can do is try, right?"

"It would be one thing if I still had the whole term to prove myself, but how much can I really accomplish in just a little more than a week?" Lani mused, talking as much to herself as to Dylan.

"A lot," Dylan answered firmly. "I know you. You're like me – you never give up on something you really want."

"Are you calling me stubborn?" Lani grinned at her friend. "But you know, you're right. Like Marta told me, Dad appreciates hard work and persistence. He had to work hard to get where he is, and he expects the same of us." She squared her shoulders. "So it's time to work hard. Time to stop feeling sorry for myself and start doing something about it."

Dylan grinned. "Now *that* sounds more like the Lani we know and love!"

For the rest of the weekend, Lani worked as hard as she could at putting her plan into action. She drew up a study schedule for herself, ignoring her friends' comments that it seemed overly ambitious. She spent Saturday night and all day Sunday at her desk, barely stopping long enough to eat, sleep, and visit the bathroom. Occasionally one of her roommates or other friends would mention that she was studying much harder than she needed to.?"You aren't a moron, Lani," as Dylan put it. "After all, if you had to study this hard all the time, your parents would be right – you don't belong here." But Lani didn't bother explaining that that wasn't the point. She didn't need to keep up this pace forever. Just long enough for her parents to get the message. All she had to do to remind herself of that was glance at her desk calendar, where a week from Wednesday was circled in red ink.

By late Monday afternoon, the pace was already starting to get to her. Lani yawned as she sat back in her desk chair, squeezing her eyes shut for a moment to rest them. The words in her history textbook were swimming in front of her eyes, no longer resembling meaningful letters and spaces so much as tiny, wriggling insects.

She opened her eyes as she heard footsteps approaching her half-open dorm room door. Glancing up, she saw Razina standing in the doorway.

"There you are!" Razina exclaimed. "We missed you at softball practice. Did you space out and forget?"

"No." Lani stifled another yawn, lifting both arms over her head to stretch her back. "I decided to skip it so I could do some extra cramming for our history test tomorrow."

"Really?" Razina looked more surprised than ever. "Um, OK. You'd better come up with a better story than that before Kari finds you, though. She was pretty mad when you didn't show."

Lani winced. Senior Kari Cohen took her position as captain of the Chestnut Hill Intramural Softball team seriously. A little *too* seriously sometimes.

"I'll think of something," she said. She checked her

watch and her eyes widened with alarm. Dinner started in less than half an hour, and she still had a lot to do. "Uh-oh – time to forget about history and get started on my French essay. Now where did I put my class notes...?"

Razina watched her for a moment, then shrugged. "See you later."

"Bye." Lani didn't bother to look up as the other girl left.

"Lani!"

Lani moaned as she felt something poking her in the spine. "Go 'way," she mumbled into her pillow. "Tired."

"Come on, get up!" The poking came again, more insistent this time. "It's nearly eight o'clock!"

That woke her up right away. "Oh, my gosh!" she exclaimed, rolling over and sitting bolt upright. She stared wildly at Honey, who was bending over her, ready to poke her again. "Are you serious? Please tell me you're not serious..."

Just then her gaze fell on the big, glowing aqua-green numbers of Malory's digital alarm clock. Sure enough, they were blinking 7:54. That meant it was actually 7:49, since Malory liked to set the clock five minutes ahead to trick herself into always being on time.

Lani leaped out of bed, almost tripping over the sheets that were wound around her leg. "Omigosh, omigosh, omigosh," she mumbled, fishing under the bed for her penny loafers. "How could I have overslept?"

Honey, who was already dressed in her school uniform and winter coat, stood back and watched Lani worriedly. "How late did you stay up last night, anyway?"

"Around two-thirty, I think." Stretching way under her bed, Lani finally located her left shoe. "I was finishing my French essay."

"Well, no wonder you overslept." Honey glanced over at the other two beds in the room. They were both empty. "But why didn't Malory or Alexandra wake you up?"

"Alexandra had an early newspaper meeting today." Lani yanked on her shoes, belatedly realizing that she was still wearing her pony-print pyjamas. Kicking off her shoes again, she rummaged through the top drawer of her dresser, looking for clean underwear. "And Malory went down to the stable to put in some extra groundwork with Tybalt before breakfast. She woke me up before she left, but I guess I fell asleep again."

"Well, you'd better hurry!" Honey said – rather unnecessarily, Lani thought. "We're supposed to be in French class in exactly ten minutes, and you know how Mme. Dubois feels about tardiness."

Lani shot her a quick glance. "No kidding," she said. "Which reminds me – you'd better get moving yourself. No sense both of us being late."

Honey looked reluctant, but she nodded. "I'll tell her you're on your way."

"Thanks."

* * *

"Detention!" Lani let out a loud groan as she and her friends left the language lab. "I can't believe Mme. D gave me detention for being a teensy bit late to class."

"Twelve minutes late," Dylan pointed out helpfully.

Lani shrugged. "Whatever. Anyway, I still can't believe she gave me detention for that. What ever happened to the idea of a warning first?" She sighed, in reality much more frustrated with herself than with her strict French teacher. "Yeah, this is really going to convince my parents that I'm doing well at Chestnut Hill," she muttered.

Honey smiled sympathetically. "Why don't we go drown your sorrows with a soda at the student centre? We have half an hour before the lunchtime lecture session starts."

"Oh, is that today?" Lani frowned. "I was planning to spend lunch period at the library writing up my science lab."

"It's today," Malory confirmed. "The speaker this time is Dr Jordan. She's really cool – I saw her on *Oprah* over Christmas break."

"Ooh, I saw that, too!" Dylan recalled enthusiastically. "And during the interview, she mentioned she used to go to Chestnut Hill! Said it gave her a wonderful start in life, or something like that."

"What does she do, exactly?" Honey asked. "I know I've heard her name, but—"

"She's a psychologist specializing in the learning process," Malory said. "She works with kids who have different kinds of developmental problems, helping work out different ways to help them, like learning a new sport and things like that."

"Cool." Honey looked interested. "Should be a good lecture, then. Come on, let's get that soda before it's time to save seats."

Lani bit her lip. Normally she enjoyed the lecture sessions with successful Chestnut Hill alumni, and this did sound like a particularly interesting topic. But this week she just didn't have time to sit around listening to any kind of speech.

She checked her watch. "You guys go ahead without me," she said. "I think I'll hit the library for a few minutes before it starts."

"What?" Dylan cried. "Come on, this is getting ridiculous! I know you're trying to get all this extra studying done to impress your parents. But what can you accomplish in the next twenty minutes?"

Lani shrugged. "It means I can get to bed tonight twenty minutes earlier," she joked weakly. Without giving the others any further chance to protest, she turned and began to jog in the direction of the library. "See you in a little while."

"Told you she'd still be here!" Malory's voice rang out across the quiet study room on the second floor of the library.

Lani looked up and smiled sheepishly at Malory and Honey, who were standing in the doorway. "Oops," she said. "Guess I lost track of the time."

That wasn't exactly true. Even before her friends had appeared, she'd been aware that the lecture was - scheduled to start in five minutes. But she hadn't wanted to break off from her studying.

"Come on," Honey urged. "Dylan went ahead to save seats for us so we can sit together."

"Why don't you guys go ahead?" Lani restlessly drummed her fingers on her open books. "Nobody will miss me – and we only have to attend four of these a term. I can skip this one."

"No way." Malory crossed her arMs "You're coming with us, and that's that."

Honey nodded. "You've been working way too hard over the past few days, not to mention skipping meals and pigging out on junk food," she said. "We're worried about you. You need to rest, or you'll go mad!"

"I'm OK." Lani brushed back her hair. "Really. You don't have to worry about me. I'm just doing what I have to do to stay here at Chestnut Hill with you guys." She chuckled wearily. "Come to think of it, maybe that *does* make me mad!"

"We'll be the judge of that," Malory said with a smile. "Now are you coming with us, or are we going to have to spend the next hour standing here staring at you?"

Lani glanced from Malory's determined face to Honey. Honey crossed her arms, too. "You heard her," the petite English girl warned. "We're ready to stand here for as long as it takes."

Lani knew when she was beaten. "All right," she

said with a sigh, standing up and gathering her books. "Let's go."

By racing at top speed through campus and cutting across the lawn and the corner of the hockey field, the three girls arrived in the auditorium of the Dawtry Arts Centre less than a minute before the lecture was scheduled to start.

"Where's Dylan?" Lani hissed as Dr Starling strode on to the stage.

"She said she'd stay near the back in case we had to sneak in late," Malory whispered back.

Honey pointed. "There she is!"

Soon the three of them were settling into their seats, which Dylan had saved by draping her coat, scarf, and gloves over them. The principal was already speaking so they couldn't talk, but Lani shot Dylan a grateful smile, and Dylan winked in return.

As Lani turned to face the stage and settled back in her seat, a wave of sadness washed over her. If she left Chestnut Hill, would her friends start saving that fourth seat for someone else?

She took her mind off that by focusing on what the principal was saying up on the stage. Dr Starling was just finishing her introduction.

"...and so I present to you yet another illustrious Chestnut Hill alumnus," she announced with a smile. "Dr Marla Jordan!"

The students applauded as Dr Jordan, a slender woman with auburn hair and an open, freckled face, walked onto the stage. After shaking Dr. Starling's hand, she took the podium.

"Good afternoon, girls," she said in a pleasant voice. "I'm here today to talk to you all about a project very close to my heart..."

After that, Lani didn't have to remind herself to pay attention, as she found herself completely caught up in Dr Jordan's talk. While Lani had never had any particular interest in the topic of child development before, Dr Jordan's engaging way of speaking made her realize how fascinating it really was. Judging by the complete silence throughout the auditorium, Lani could tell she wasn't the only one hooked. Using a series of photos and other visual aids, the psychologist started off by demonstrating the different ways she and her colleagues tried to help children with developmental problems achieve their full potential.

"We try to give the children whatever will help them the most," Dr Jordan explained, clicking her remote control so that a photo of a smiling boy holding a basketball flashed up on the screen behind her. "Sometimes that means special schooling. Other times, it means getting them involved in a new sport. I've seen kids make truly incredible progress after learning to swim, ride horses, or play basketball."

Dylan nudged Lani in the side. "Ride horses!" she whispered. "How cool is that?"

Lani nodded and smiled, then returned her attention to the speaker. After describing a little more of her research, Dr Jordan went on to talk about her role on the board of a charity called AllSports.

"AllSports raises funds to help children with developmental issues get involved in some of the different recreational activities I've been telling you about," she said.

She clicked to another photo, this one showing a group of young girls with their arms slung around one another's shoulders, big smiles on their faces. One of the girls in the front was holding a volleyball.

"Working with the charity has been very rewarding. There's nothing better than seeing a child change from sad and withdrawn to happy and active right in front of your eyes, or helping a teenager realize she can accomplish much more than she ever imagined. And of course, volunteering is yet another of the values I learned right here at Chestnut Hill. I still have great memories of the charity projects my dorm got involved with. Trust me, these experiences are something you'll carry with you all your life, just as much as your education and friendships and everything else you get from being at school."

Lani nodded. Each half-term, a different dorm was expected to run a charity event for the whole school. Her dorm's turn was coming up – in fact, the initial planning meeting was scheduled for that very Thursday.

At least that means I'll get to help out with our fund-raiser before I leave, Lani thought rather wistfully as the lecture wrapped up. *It's no wonder people like Dr Jordan are willing to come back and talk to us. Chestnut Hill is such an amazing place. Where else would we have the chance to do such cool things and learn from such interesting speakers? I wonder if they do stuff like this at that school in California.*

She shuddered as she realized that, all too soon, she might get the chance to find out.

Chapter Six

"Wait!" Lani protested, grabbing the edge of her desk as Dylan yanked on her arm. "I only have two more pages to go in this chapter."

"It can wait until *after* the meeting." Honey reached over and flipped Lani's history textbook shut. "Now come along – don't make us tickle you!"

"That threat only works on you, Honey." But Lani let go and stood up, knowing resistance was futile. Besides, no matter how worried she was about finishing her history homework, she didn't want to miss the dorm meeting about the upcoming community service project.

"So do any of us have any brilliant ideas to suggest tonight?" Dylan asked as the four of them headed toward the upperclassmen's lounge, where the Adams seniors had called the meeting. "We have to make sure we seventh-graders look good, you know." She wrinkled her nose. "Especially since I overheard Lynsey and Patience muttering about a fashion show."

"No surprises there." Lani shook her head. "And

what cause do they want to raise money for – fashion victims?"

Malory laughed. "Sounds about right," she said.

When the four friends entered the upperclass lounge, most of the dorm residents were already there. "Great," Dylan muttered, nudging Lani in the ribs as they surveyed the crowded lounge from the doorway. "Thanks to you, we're stuck with standing room only."

"Sorry," Lani whispered back, even though she was pretty sure Dylan was kidding. She was right, though – people were sitting five or six to a couch and two to a chair, while others perched on windowsills or sprawled on the floor. Lani noticed Lynsey and Patience sitting together on an upholstered chair right up front.

Lani and her friends found an open spot to sit down on the carpet just as Noel Cousins stood up to call the meeting to order. Noel was the dorm prefect and also the co-captain of the senior jumping team. At the moment her thick auburn hair was pulled back in a casual ponytail and she was holding a clipboard.

"As you know," Noel began as all eyes turned to her, "it's our turn here in Adams to run the next fund-raiser at Chestnut Hill. I know we're all excited about this" – she paused and smiled as several ragged cheers rang out from around the room – "and I know a lot of people remember our last Adams fund-raiser, which was a big hit."

"What did you do?" Lani called out, curious.

"A talent show," replied a junior named Rosie Williams, who was sitting nearby. "It was awesome!"

Noel nodded. "We raised more money than any other dorm last year," she said. "So naturally, we want to make sure this new event is something special, too – *Adams* special!"

This time more people cheered. Lani grinned, caught up in the general enthusiasm. "A talent show does sound cool," she commented to her friends. "Wish I'd been here for that."

Noel raised her hands for silence. "So I hope you all brought your best ideas," she said, her face dimpling into a smile. "Please raise your hand if you have something to suggest. We also need ideas for which charity we want to benefit."

The first girl to speak was a sophomore named Natasha Kapinsky. "Why don't we do another talent show?" she suggested. "I mean, it worked so well the first time – why mess with success?"

A few people cheered, but more shrugged or looked underwhelmed. Lani's first thought was that they should do something new, though she was already imagining various fun sketches and songs she and her friends could perform.

"We'll take that idea into consideration, Natasha," Noel said diplomatically, making a quick note on her clipboard. "But I'm sure we can come up with something new and even better if we tap into that great Adams creativity. Who's next?"

A senior suggested holding a winter carnival. A junior named Rachel Goodhart proposed a recipe contest to benefit famine relief. And sure enough,

Lynsey raised her hand to suggest a fashion show, complete with various details about using her mother's contacts in the fashion world to procure the loan of stylish outfits, or help run a modeling talent search throughout the school. She even volunteered to approach some big-name celebrities and ask them to donate items for a fashion auction.

"It would be fabulous!" Patience spoke up eagerly, supporting Lynsey's idea. "Like instead of a walk-a-thon, it'll be a fashion-a-thon!"

"We can't let that idea win," Lani whispered to her friends. "Lynsey practically took over the auction for the library last term – the last thing we want is another school event that's totally focused on her!"

Dylan looked torn; even though she was the last person to praise anything Lynsey and Patience came up with, she enjoyed fashion and shopping almost as much as they did. "I guess you're right," she said reluctantly. "It would totally be Lynsey World. But none of the other ideas are exactly blowing me away."

"We need to come up with something better, then," Honey murmured back. "Something original that hasn't ever been done before."

Dylan shrugged. "Yeah. But what? It should be something really fun – maybe some kind of sports tournament? Basketball, volleyball?"

Lani glanced at her. "Volleyball..." she echoed thoughtfully.

At that moment a freshman sitting across the room raised her hand. "We could do a litter-a-thon," she suggested. "Get people to sponsor us picking up litter around the county."

Lynsey wrinkled her nose. "Are you kidding?" she said before Noel or anyone else could respond. "Who wants to pick up old beer bottles and junk when we could do my fashion show idea? We can make it benefit, like, some local shelter that needs clothes or something."

"Ooh! Or how about that charity that provides interview and work clothes to people trying to get off welfare?" someone else called out. "I saw something about them on, like, *Dateline*. Or maybe it was on *Dr Phil*."

"Hmm. That's a good cause," Noel said, making another note. "Should we take a vote, or does anyone else have any—"

"Wait!" Lani shot up her hand. "I have an idea!"

"You do?" Dylan said in surprise.

Lani climbed to her feet. "When Dylan mentioned volleyball just now, it reminded me of Dr Jordan's talk," she said. "She's on the board of the charity called AllSports, remember? Why don't we do something to benefit them?"

"Hey, that's a great idea!" someone called out.

Lynsey didn't look particularly impressed. "That's a nice group, I suppose," she said. "But it doesn't really go with the whole fashion show theme. Anyway, it can't compare with the group we were just talking about. That actually helps people get jobs and stuff." She shrugged. "All Dr Jordan's group does is help kids learn to play tennis or whatever."

"No, it doesn't," Lani protested. "AllSports is much more than that. Don't you remember how Dr Jordan showed pictures and told stories about how much her work has helped kids with developmental problems? It's not just about teaching them to play sports, it's about teaching them life skills and achieving their potential and stuff."

She paused, shooting her friends a quick glance as her nerve started to fail her. After all, arguing with Lynsey was one thing, but right now she had the attention of her whole dorm! Malory grinned encouragingly, and Dylan gave her a thumbs-up.

"Anyway," Lani went on, reckoning she'd got this far so she might as well finish, "I'm not saying the other charities we're talking about aren't great, too. But this is a way we could make a difference to people our own age. Chestnut Hill gives us all so much – not only the chance to learn from top teachers, but also to get involved in riding and other sports, to hear great speakers like Dr. Jordan. It helps us to become well-rounded people. Dr Jordan's programme does the same thing with these kids, right? She helps them overcome their personal issues, and gives them something else in their lives to enjoy. That seems pretty important to me." She stopped talking since she was practically out of breath and waited, wondering if she'd just made a complete idiot of herself.

To her surprise, there was a burst of cheers and applause. "Way to go, Lani!" Dylan hooted.

"Great speech, Lani." Noel smiled at her. "And I'm

sold on your idea. We'll definitely put AllSports on the list. So what's your idea for the fund-raiser?"

"What?" Lani blinked, realizing that the entire dorm was gazing at her expectantly. Even Lynsey was silent, waiting to see what she had to say.

Normally Lani wasn't a shy person. But she could feel her face turning red as she searched her mind for something to say. She hadn't thought beyond her initial impulse to bring up Dr Jordan's group.

"I – uh – " she began uncertainly.

"I know!" Malory burst out. "Sorry to interrupt whatever you were going to say, Lani. But I just had a great idea. Chestnut Hill is known for its incredible riding programme – why not use that somehow to raise money for AllSports? After all, Dr. Jordan mentioned riding as one of the sports she uses – it's a perfect fit!"

"You mean like a horse show?" another senior guessed.

Noel looked interested. "Good thinking, Malory," she said. "That really would be a nice fit for Chestnut Hill."

"I suppose it's not a bad idea," Lynsey admitted, as if any ideas needed her seal of approval before they could get accepted. "We could put on a riding demonstration like we did for Homecoming, then have a competition between the different dorms" She smiled smugly as she glanced around at the various members of the junior and senior jumping teams who were present. "Adams would definitely kick butt."

Patience's eyes widened. "Ooh! Or how about

fashion on horseback?" she exclaimed. "We could all show off the new show clothes we got for Christmas – I've been dying for a chance to wear my new Grand Prix jacket."

"Sure," Lynsey said agreed halfheartedly. "That could be part of the show."

Lani glanced at her friends in alarm. For a second she'd been thrilled by Malory's idea to make the fund-raiser something horse related. But now that Lynsey and Patience were taking over the idea, it was starting to sound way too formal and competitive.

Dylan raised her hand. "A horse show sounds cool and all," she said to the group. "But is a regular show really going to be interesting to the whole school? Maybe we should come up with something more original, something that would be fun for the spectators as well as the riders. Like a gymkhana or something."

"A gym-what?" Senior Faith Holby-Travis, who didn't ride, looked confused. "What's that?"

Before anyone else could answer, Lynsey waved a hand dismissively. "It's just a thing for kids with ponies that aren't well-bred enough to show properly," she said. "You know – pony clubbers and those types. They do kiddie stuff like egg-and-spoon races and obstacle courses and stuff. Probably barrel racing, too." She shrugged. "They don't tackle any real disciplines like jumping or dressage."

Lani rolled her eyes. Leave it to Lynsey to make something fun like a gymkhana sound so pathetic. It irritated her enough to speak out again – just as a new idea popped into her head.

"I've got an even better idea," she called out impulsively. "And it's all thanks to Lynsey mentioning barrel racing, actually. Why don't we go all the way and have a rodeo?"

There was a moment of rather startled silence. "A rodeo?" Noel echoed uncertainly. "Interesting idea. What do you have in mind?"

This time Lani's mind didn't fail her. Ideas were bubbling inside her head faster than she could express them. "OK, it wouldn't be like a full rodeo," she admitted. "I mean, we couldn't pull off stuff like bull riding or calf roping. But we could still call it a Rodeo Day, and make it a day of Western-style riding. We could have barrel racing and pole bending for starters, and maybe a reining demonstration or clinic – reining's getting way more popular."

"I love it!" A junior named Helen Savage, who was from Texas and rode on the senior jumping team, stood up and grinned. "I think the rodeo idea is awesome. We could get the riding staff involved, too, since they'd have to help us out. It would be something most people don't get to do very often, since Western riding isn't in the curriculum here. We can have fun with the whole Western theme."

Lani nodded, grateful for the support. "We could have other Western stuff that everyone can take part in, even people who didn't want to ride. Like maybe getting one of those Old West–style photographers to take pictures of people dressed in Western costumes."

"Or Western-style carnival games," someone Lani couldn't see called out.

"Yeah," another girl added. "And maybe someone could give a clinic on throwing a lasso!"

A lot of people chuckled at that idea. Lani glanced around the room, still not quite sure how the majority of people were going to respond to her proposal. She was thrilled to see that most girls were looking intrigued and thoughtful, while others were already looking downright enthusiastic.

"Wait a second." Lynsey's voice cut through the murmurs of approval. "We aren't seriously considering this stupid idea, are we? Why would we mess around with barrels and ropes and stuff when we have all the facilities to put on a first-class hunter-jumper show? It's crazy."

"Yeah," Patience spoke up. "Besides, who wants to do all that Western stuff?"

"I do!" Noel raised her hand. "I think it sounds like a blast. What does everybody else think?"

Noel's enthusiasm – and Lani's – seemed to be contagious. Within seconds, hands were shooting into the air all over the room.

Lani glanced over at Lynsey and Patience, whose hands stayed firmly by their sides. But as it became clear that the tide of popular opinion was in danger of turning against them, Lynsey shrugged.

"Whatever," she said. "Majority rules, I suppose. But if we're going to do this, let's at least do it with some class. I'd be happy to volunteer for the hospitality committee. My mother works with a fantastic caterer in DC who could probably come up with, you know, cow-shaped canapés or whatever."

"Canapés at a rodeo?" Dylan protested. "People are going to expect some good old Western chuckwagon-style grub. Like burgers, and, um – " She glanced at Lani for help.

"Ribs, of course," Lani said immediately. "And chili. We could even include a chili cook-off if we want – that would use Rachel's idea, too." She grinned at the junior who had suggested the recipe contest.

Rachel smiled back. "Cool! I'd be happy to take charge of that," she volunteered.

"Excellent." Noel started scribbling notes frantically as other people shouted out ideas for the rodeo. "There's going to be a ton of work for everyone. But this could be our best fund-raiser ever!" She glanced at Lani and grinned. "And since you're the expert in this area, Lani, I guess that makes you the head of the Activities Committee."

"Me?" Somehow, Lani hadn't expected that. Normally the main committees for dorm projects were run by the juniors and seniors, with the younger students playing supporting roles. She gulped, visions of that unfinished history chapter dancing in her head. This project sounded like it was going to be pretty time-consuming, and she barely had time to eat and sleep as it was, thanks to the rigorous study schedule she'd set for herself.

"Thanks for the original idea, Lani!" Noel concluded.

The rest of the room murmured "thanks" and "congratulations" with a few whistles thrown in.

Lani blushed and grinned, her concerns swept away in the general rush of excitement. If there was any cause worth taking time away from her studies, this seemed like it. "Thanks, guys," she said. "I'll do my best to make you proud!"

After all, she thought as she hurried forward to join Noel at the front of the room, *who needs sleep?*

Chapter Seven

"Line up, everyone." Ms Carmichael clapped her hands for attention. "We're going to do something special today."

Lynsey frowned as she brought Bluegrass to a smooth, square halt by the rail of the outdoor arena. It was an unseasonably warm January day, and Ms Carmichael had announced that they would hold that day's lesson outside to give the ponies and riders a break from the indoor arena.

"Let me guess," Lynsey said, just loudly enough that the riding instructor couldn't hear her but most of the other girls in the intermediate class could. "More *eventing* stuff."

She pronounced "eventing" with the same disdain she always did when the subject came up. Lani sighed. Lynsey had made it pretty clear over the past two weeks that she wasn't particularly interested in expanding her horizons to include cross-country riding.

"What's the matter?" Dylan taunted softly. "Afraid

your fancy show pony can't handle the challenge? Or is it his *rider* who can't cut it?"

Lynsey rolled her eyes. "Very mature, Dylan," she snapped. "I just think it's foolish to waste time on that yahoo sport when we could be practising stuff that will help us win the Junior All Schools Trophy this year."

Lani glanced over to see if Ms Carmichael had heard any of their exchange. The instructor seemed unaware of the conversation going on at the end of the ring as she fiddled around with a tack trunk just inside the arena fence.

"Here you go," Ms Carmichael said over her shoulder. "Let's see if this gives you a hint..."

She straightened up and turned around, hoisting into view a slightly battered Western saddle. The cinch was wrapped around the dusty horn, while the fenders with their padded leather stirrups swung almost to the ground.

Lani gasped. "Where did that come from?" she exclaimed.

Ms Carmichael grinned. "I brought it with me from Kentucky," she said. "It's one of the saddles I used to pony horses when I worked at one of the local tracks for a while."

"What's it doing here now?" Lynsey asked with a touch of alarm.

"A little bird told me about the Adams Rodeo Day fund-raiser." Ms Carmichael chuckled. "Since some of you East Coasters have probably never seen a saddle with a horn up close, I thought it might be helpful to have a little demonstration."

"Cool!" Dylan called out. "You mean you're going to ride for us in that saddle?"

Lani grinned delightedly. She and the other students rarely got the chance to see Ms Carmichael ride, unless they happened to catch her after hours schooling her own horse, the handsome young Thoroughbred cross named Quince.

"Not me," Ms Carmichael said, crushing Lani's hopes. "I'm going to ask Lani to ride for us in this saddle."

Lani stared at her. "What? Me?"

"Why not?" Malory spoke up with a smile. "You've probably done more Western riding than the rest of this school put together."

Lynsey rolled her eyes. "Like *that's* something to brag about."

Ignoring her, Lani narrowed her eyes at the saddle Ms Carmichael was holding. Her heart had started to race with excitement. "Will that saddle fit Colorado? And what if he doesn't understand what I'm doing when I try to ride him Western?"

"How do you think he got the name Colorado?" Ms Carmichael teased. "He was born on a ranch in your home state, and, according to his papers, spent the first four years of his life there learning from Colorado cowboys. As for your first question, there's only one way to find out..."

A few minutes later, Lani was pulling the cinch knot tighter and adjusting the fenders to the right length. Colorado stood calmly with his head down and his eyes half closed, looking for all the world like a patient little cow pony in an old Western print.

"It fits perfectly!" Lani declared, stepping back to gaze at the saddle. "How lucky is that?"

"Fabulous," Lynsey pronounced in a bored voice. She had dropped her reins on Bluegrass's withers, and the pretty roan pony was standing quietly with one hind foot cocked. "Colorado looks like he's been wearing that thing all his life."

Lani knew the other girl didn't mean that as a compliment, but she let it pass, merely smiling as she heard Dylan hiss "Snob!" under her breath. Moving to Colorado's head, she made one last check of the pelham bridle, the closest thing the Chestnut Hill tack room had to a Western curb, which Ms Carmichael had fetched to replace Colorado's usual D-ring snaffle.

Then she turned to Ms Carmichael. "So what do you want me to do?"

"Whatever you feel like," the teacher replied. "You already warmed him up under English tack, so why don't you just hop on and show us a few moves?" She glanced at the other girls. "Y'all don't mind watching for a while, do you?"

"I can't wait!" Honey declared.

Dylan and Malory nodded, along with two of the other three members of the class, Paris Mackenzie of Curie and Heidi Johnson of Potter. Nadia Smith, who lived in Granville House, merely exchanged a shrug and an eye-roll with Lynsey but kept quiet. Lani knew that the two girls, along with several of their friends, were decidedly unimpressed by Ali Carmichael's Midwest background.

I guess they think anyone who isn't from a few blue-blood approved areas of the East Coast might as well be from Timbuktu, Lani mused.

"Ready to hop on?" Ms Carmichael interrupted her thoughts.

"Definitely!" Lani swung aboard, unable to resist a grin at the familiar feel of sinking into the soft leather seat of a Western saddle. Picking up the reins, she unbuckled them.

"What are you doing, Lani?" asked sharp-eyed Heidi.

"A lot of Western riders use split reins," Lani replied. "I'm just trying to be authentic."

Ms Carmichael nodded. "Notice how she's holding those reins, class," she said as Lani asked Colorado to walk forward. "In English riding, we talk a lot about proper contact. In Western riding, their version of contact is merely the weight of the reins. See how there's slack? With a true Western curb bit, the horse would still be receiving plenty of input – an English level of contact would be too harsh. Also note that she's holding both reins in one hand. Western riding developed that way because it left one hand free for roping or whatever else a cowboy needed to do while on horseback."

"Hey, check it out," Lani called excitedly as she steered the buckskin pony around the ring. "Colorado neck reins!"

For the benefit of her classmates, she demonstrated

by moving her hand exaggeratedly from side to side. As the right rein touched Colorado's neck, the pony turned to the left. When Lani moved her hand again, this time bringing the left rein against Colorado's neck, he turned back to the right. She steered him in a figure eight, and then a small circle.

Good boy, Colorado, she thought as she guided him through a few more figures. *I always knew you were the smartest pony in the world!*

"That's pretty cool," Dylan commented. "You look like one of those reiners I saw on TV once."

"Where was that, the redneck channel?" Lynsey muttered.

Ms Carmichael frowned. "Enough, Lynsey," she said. Then she returned her attention to Lani. "Speaking of reining, any chance you can show us some moves?"

"Sure. I took a few lessons a couple of years ago. I'm probably pretty rusty, though..."

Taking a deep breath, Lani asked for a canter – known in Western terminology as a lope. She rode to the far end of the arena, giving herself some space. Then she steered Colorado in a big circle at an easy lope, before urging him on to a faster pace and making a smaller circle. Other than the fact that she was on a long rein, that part wasn't any different than their usual English flatwork, and the buckskin pony had no trouble at all. She could hear Ms Carmichael talking to the others about what she was doing, explaining each move.

Next she turned in at the far end of the arena, this

time aiming the pony down the middle in a straight line. About halfway down, she asked for a sudden halt, leaning way back in the saddle and exaggerating her aids.

Colorado responded immediately, screeching to a halt so suddenly that he slid forward a few inches, sending up a cloud of dust.

"OK, that wasn't exactly a real sliding stop," Lani called apologetically to the class, leaning forward to give the pony a quick pat. "Just pretend we skidded forward about ten feet, OK? Now I'm going to try a rollback..."

She felt a little more confident about that, since it was similar to a move they practised for jumper courses. Sure enough, Colorado obediently spun around on his haunches from the halt, then loped off easily in the opposite direction.

"Good boy!" Lani cried gleefully. At the other end of the ring she changed leads and did one more circle in the opposite direction, then tried another sliding stop. This time Colorado seemed to catch on to what she wanted, slamming on the brakes more abruptly than ever. While it wouldn't have won any points at a real reining competition, he did skid forward a little more on this attempt, and Lani's heart swelled with pride. Though Colorado had his quirks, she'd never ridden a horse that tried so hard to please his rider. It was just one of the many things she loved about him.

Next, Lani asked the pony to back up, jiggling the reins a little to encourage him to speed up. Colorado scooted backward about five or six steps. It wasn't anything like the calm, collected moves he did so well in equitation classes, which was just as Lani had intended. When she asked him to halt again, he did so instantly, standing squarely but on the muscle, waiting for her next command.

Instead of asking him to do anything else, she leaned forward to give him another pat. The pony relaxed at once, putting his head down and blowing out a sigh.

"You're the best, buddy," she whispered, smiling as he flicked back one ear to catch her voice. Then she nudged him into a walk, heading back toward the group. "That was fun!" she declared. "OK, what next? Should Colorado and I try a little trail pattern or something?" Lani loved trail classes and how they were like an obstacle course on horseback. Trail classes had developed as a way to practise skills needed on a trail ride – stuff like opening and closing gates, stepping over logs, sidepassing, and strong communication between horse and rider.

"We could do that at some point. A trail pattern challenge would be a great event for Rodeo Day, but for now, I was thinking of something a little more exciting," Ms Carmichael said. "Something like, say, barrel racing?"

Lani grinned. "I'm game," she said. It had been a while since she'd had an opportunity to run barrels, but she still remembered how much fun it was. "What are we going to use for barrels?"

"Already on it." Ms Carmichael nodded.

Glancing toward the side of the ring, Lani saw Sarah and Kelly pushing along a pair of the big, brightly colored plastic water barrels that normally stood under the eaves of the barns to catch rain runoff.

A few of the ponies snorted and danced in alarm as the two young women rolled the barrels into the arena. Kelly started setting them in place while Sarah hurried off to fetch a third barrel. Before long they had set up a passable course – the three barrels set up in a broad triangle at one end of the ring.

Lani felt adrenaline surge through her. "Should I trot through it first, or what?" she asked the instructor. "I haven't done this for ages, and it may be Colorado's first time ever."

"I think you can give it a try at canter if you're comfortable with that," Ms Carmichael said. "I suspect Colorado might know what he's doing. If not, you can always slow down or pull out. OK? Ready, set..."

Lani barely heard the *GO!* as she and Colorado exploded from a halt into a full gallop. So much for a canter! Lani could feel the little quarter horse's powerful hindquarters gather beneath him with each stride, like a jet engine taking off. Lani leaned forward, not worrying about her heels coming up or her elbows flapping out as she urged him on. Equitation didn't matter in barrel racing as long as you stayed aboard – the only important thing was speed!

"Steady," she whispered as they approached the first barrel, though the word was lost in the wind whooshing around her ears.

Still, Colorado seemed to hear her. He collected his stride as she guided him around it in a clockwise direction, looking for the spot where they could safely start to turn, also known as "the pocket." As they came back around, his hooves skidding in the sand, Lani felt his shoulder lightly bump the barrel. It wasn't enough to knock it over, but it did make the pony hesitate.

"Go, go, go!" she cried, urging him on with her legs and seat.

Colorado surged across the arena toward the next barrel in the cloverleaf pattern. His ears flattened against his head as he crossed the open area, but they popped forward as they neared the next barrel and, once again, Lani asked him to slow and focus. She collected him just enough to ask him to switch leads, which he did at once.

This time they hit the pocket perfectly. Lani lifted her rein to keep Colorado from dropping his shoulder, and the pony spun easily around the barrel on his left lead, kicking up clouds of dust with his hooves. On the other side, he dug in and raced forward as Lani aimed him toward the third and final barrel.

Lani was vaguely aware that her classmates were cheering as she reached the last barrel at the far end of the arena. But she blocked it out, focusing only on the horse beneath her as she gathered him for one last careful turn.

"Good boy!" she shouted as he came around the other side. "Now go!"

She flip-flopped the ends of the reins against his

shoulders, and Colorado galloped across the arena at full tilt, slowing only when Lani sat up after they'd crossed the imaginary finish line.

Lani could feel a big grin stretching across her face. "Whoo-hoo!" she crowed between gasps for air. "That was fun!"

"Nice work!" Ms Carmichael said. "It's too bad we didn't have a timer – I bet that was a pretty competitive run." She turned toward the rest of the class. "I'm guessing that anything around seventeen seconds would be a good time for a course this size. Of course, if Lani had knocked over a barrel, that would mean five seconds added on to her time. Just as knocking down a jump usually means points or seconds off in a jumper class."

"Seventeen seconds? I bet Lani just did it in ten," Dylan exclaimed loyally. "She's a natural at this stuff. Colorado, too."

Lynsey didn't have much to say, but everyone else crowded forward, eager to talk about what they'd just seen. If they'd already been looking forward to Rodeo Day, seeing Lani ride the barrel pattern had made them more enthusiastic than ever.

Lani was still beaming a few minutes later as she led Colorado into his stall. "You were great today, buddy," she told him as she slipped off his bridle and rubbed his favorite itchy spot under his chin. "First I'm going to sponge you off, then I'll put on your cooler and we'll go for a walk to find you some grass while you dry off."

As she undid the cinch and lifted the Western saddle

off his back, she found herself humming. That day's riding class had been a lot of fun; it had helped remind her how much she enjoyed Western riding as well as English.

Suddenly reality came crashing down on her as she realized it had reminded her of something else: just how much fun she always had at Chestnut Hill. She hoisted the saddle onto the top of the half-door and turned back to give Colorado a big hug around the neck, barely noticing his sweaty coat. She buried her hands in his mane and crossed her fingers, hoping all that fun wasn't going to end way sooner than she'd planned.

Over the next few days, Ms Carmichael offered several extracurricular Western riding classes during free periods. Lani and her friends took full advantage of them, even though Lani couldn't help fretting over the time she was losing from her studies. There weren't enough Western saddles to go around, but everyone got the chance to sit in Ms Carmichael's old saddle at least once and to learn some reining moves, practise their trail patterns, and try Western Pleasure-style riding. Kelly even found some real metal barrels to create a barrel racing course, though for the moment Ms Carmichael wouldn't let anyone except Lani try it at any gait faster than a slow, collected canter.

The hours seemed to pass like minutes – Lani couldn't believe how much she needed to get done each day. Between riding and her other classes, planning for the fund-raiser, and keeping up with her homework, she was barely aware of the days slipping by. She was so caught up in the excitement about Rodeo Day that she scarcely had time to worry about her future at Chestnut Hill, though she couldn't help the odd moment of anxiety – especially when she looked at the big red circle on her calendar marking the day of her parents' meeting with Dr Starling. More than once, she wondered if she should give something up – like being the head of the Activities Committee. Could she really handle that on top of everything else?

She wasn't sure. But she had to try. Everyone was counting on her, and so she just buckled down and did it.

Suddenly it was Wednesday. As soon as Lani woke up, she got a knot in her stomach. *Today's the day,* she thought as she sat up and rubbed the sleep out of her eyes. *The day my fate is decided.*

She tried not to fret over it during her morning classes, but by the time she headed to riding class that afternoon, the knot in her stomach felt about the same size as one of the bales of hay stacked in the barn aisle. Her friends were sympathetic – they knew exactly how important this day was – but she hardly took in their concerned comments and words of encouragement. In fact, she was so distracted that she tried to put in Colorado's bit backward, and almost forgot to put on her helmet before mounting.

But finally she was in the ring warming up. The familiar routine was soothing, and she felt herself relax.

It was a jumping day, and Ms Phillips, the school's jumping coach, was running the class. She had set up a small course during the warm-up period, and asked the riders to go through it one at a time. While waiting for her turn, Lani found herself tensing up again. Even Colorado seemed to notice – earlier in the class he'd been calm and good-tempered, but now he started to dance restlessly.

"Easy, boy," she murmured. "It's OK."

But the words rang hollow in her ears. By the end of the day, she would know exactly how "OK" things really were. Would all her worry turn out to be for nothing? Or would her worst nightmare come true – would her parents announce that she really did have to say goodbye to Chestnut Hill, to her friends, to Colorado, for good? She wasn't sure she could stand the suspense for another second, let alone another hour.

All I can do is argue my case and hope for the best, she told herself, taking a jittery breath and then blowing it out so hard that Colorado's mane fluttered. *I just hope I didn't blow it by getting too caught up in this Rodeo Day thin...*

"Ms Hernandez! Are you with us?"

The coach's annoyed voice broke through her daze, and she realized that Ms Phillips must have called her for her turn more than once. "Oh – sorry!" she blurted out, gathering up her reins so quickly that Colorado snorted in surprise. Giving him a quick pat on the withers to apologize, she kicked him into a trot and headed for the start of the course.

Colorado's canter felt a bit choppy during their opening circle, but by the time they approached the first fence, an inviting cross rail, he had regained his focus even if his rider hadn't. He popped over it easily, ears pricked toward the vertical coming up next.

The pony's steady stride helped to ease Lani's nerves. Letting out the breath she hadn't even realized she was holding, she did her best to concentrate on what she was doing. Shortening Colorado's canter, she found a perfect line to approach the vertical, and they sailed over.

Immediately after the fence she asked for the lead change, expecting Colorado to swap cleanly just as he'd done on the barrel course over the past few days. But she'd forgotten that, while his right-to-left change was all but automatic, his left-to-right one could be a bit sticky. The pony slowed and humped his back, but maintained the left lead into the turn. Lani asked again, more forcefully this time.

Colorado obeyed, though the change was sloppy and included a small buck. Not letting that rattle her – it was hardly the first time it had happened – Lani focused on the next line, which was coming up fast. They faced another vertical, followed by five strides to an oxer. Lani could already see her spot to the vertical, but unfortunately the lead change battle had left Colorado strung out and scattered, and she couldn't collect him quickly enough to adjust his stride. They ended up chipping in at the vertical and landing short on the other side.

Lani had only a split second to decide what to do next. She could try to collect him further, doing the line in six instead of five, or she could push for the five, relying on the pony's natural forwardness to help her out.

When in doubt, ride forward. That was one of Ms Carmichael's favourite pieces of advice, and Lani decided to follow it.

She pushed Colorado through the next couple of strides. He picked up steam quickly, and for a second Lani smiled, certain that they were going to pull it off.

Then she caught a flash of movement out of the corner of her eye. Shifting her gaze, she saw a tall, dark-haired, broad-shouldered man and a petite, pretty blonde woman standing at the rail with Ms Carmichael beside them. It was Lani's parents, and they were watching her ride!

She gasped, completely forgetting what she was doing. The reins slid through her hands, and Colorado shook his head crossly. He was a good jumper, but he required a strong rider. When he sensed Lani was no longer focused, he gave a small buck of irritation and swerved to the left.

Yanking on the right rein to bring him back into line, Lani realized with horror that they were now a stride and a half from the oxer. She booted Colorado hard to ask for the long spot, simultaneously preparing herself for an unbalanced takeoff.

Colorado launched himself at the oxer. He scrabbled wildly at the air, and Lani felt her feet bounce out of the stirrups. If it had been another cross rail or vertical, they might have made it over. But the back rail of the oxer was too high and they crashed right through it, sending the pole flying. Snorting with alarm, Colorado landed and plunged to the right, while Lani went flying off to the left.

For a split second, she saw the arena spinning as she tumbled through the air – ground, sky, ground, sky…

Then she hit the sand with a thud, and everything went black.

Chapter Eight

Lani opened her eyes. For a moment she was confused – instead of the tiled white ceiling of her dorm room, she saw blue afternoon sky with a few fluffy winter clouds scudding across it. She had the disturbing feeling she wasn't lying in bed after all…

Then her father's face came into the frame, his strong features creased with worry. "I think she's coming around," he said.

Lani blinked as her memory returned in a rush – the oxer, that flying leap?…

"Ugh," she groaned as pain shot through her entire body, finally settling in her right wrist. She started to push herself upright.

Ms Phillips bent over and put a hand on her shoulder to stop her. "Don't move!" the jumping coach ordered.

"Stay where you are, Lani," Ms Carmichael warned more gently, stepping forward and peering down at her. "The school nurse is on her way."

"I'm OK," Lani protested weakly. But she obeyed,

lying back and closing her eyes.

Her wrist throbbed, letting her know in no uncertain terms that she wasn't OK. She could feel tiny stones poking into her in various places, and a chilly breeze suggested that the right knee of her brand-new jodhpurs had been shredded.

In the background, she could hear the murmur of voices and the soft snorts and stamps of ponies. "Is she all right?" Honey's concerned voice rose over the others.

"I'm sure she'll be fine," Ms Phillips said, though her shaky voice belied her soothing words. "Dylan should be back soon with Nurse O'Connor. Everything will be OK."

Lani wasn't so sure about that. In fact, she couldn't remember a time when things had looked worse. Her wrist was in agony, and worse yet, she could hear her mother and father talking quietly about her accident from just a few feet away. First her mother's anxious voice said something about the jump falling over, and then her father mentioned Colorado…

Colorado! With a flash of terror, she remembered how he'd flailed his way through the jump. She turned her head, trying to spot her pony. Was he OK?

To her relief, she saw that Malory had dismounted and was walking him in a circle, talking to him soothingly. Colorado walked along with her easily, with no hint of lameness or other distress, and Lani breathed out a sigh of relief.

She turned her head back again and allowed her

eyes to close. She didn't want her parents to include her in their conversation just yet. After what they'd just seen, she was sure they'd decide to yank her out of Chestnut Hill right then and there.

"Lani, sweetie." Her mother's voice made her reluctantly open her eyes. Mrs Hernandez was gazing down at her with deep concern. "Can you hear me? How many fingers am I holding up?"

"I'm OK, Mom." Lani lifted her left arm and brushed away her mother's hand. "I'm sure I can sit up – only my wrist hurts..."

But her parents, Ms Phillips, and Ms Carmichael insisted that she stay still until the school nurse arrived. Fortunately Lani didn't have long to wait before Ms O'Connor was next to her in the ring, poking and prodding and asking questions.

"I think she's OK, except for that wrist. We'll need to take a closer look at that back at the clinic," the nurse announced at last. She helped Lani into a sitting position. "Lucky she was wearing her approved helmet – you should replace that now that it's done its job protecting your noggin from the hard ground."

"I will," Lani promised, reaching up with her good hand to unhook the safety harness on her helmet. "I have a spare back in my dorm."

She could see her classmates watching her with worried eyes. Some of the girls were still mounted, though Malory, Honey, and Dylan were on the ground. Malory was holding Colorado's reins, while Honey held Tybalt's along with Falcon's.

"Wait," Lani blurted out. "I need to untack Colorado."

"I'm sure your classmates can take care of that for you, Lani," he father said, helping her to her feet. "Let's get you to the clinic."

Lani glanced up at him, trying to read his expression. But he didn't meet her eyes as he put an arm around her shoulders and steered her toward the gate. She felt that old knot in her stomach return, bigger and more uncomfortable than ever. Her first fall at Chestnut Hill, and her parents just happened to be watching... Did they need any more evidence that she'd be better off in California?

Less than half an hour later, Ms O'Connor was making final adjustments to the sling on Lani's wrist while addressing her parents, who were sitting in the visitors' chairs in one of the school clinic's exam rooms

"She's lucky it's not broken," the nurse said. "But she'll still have to be careful for the next couple of weeks."

Commander Hernandez nodded, straightening the collar of his dark wool jacket. "I'm sure she'll follow your instructions to the letter, Ms O'Connor."

Lani sat there clutching her bandaged wrist, feeling like the Invisible Girl as the adults talked over her head. Had they forgotten she was there? Or did it just feel that way?

Ms O'Connor smiled at Commander Hernandez,

then gazed sternly at Lani. "Keep this sling on during waking hours, and no sports for at least two weeks," she said. "The riding faculty won't question that, of course, and I'll give you a note for Ms Feist. And be careful about everyday movements, too – getting dressed, carrying your lunch tray, and so forth. You might need some help from your friends for a while."

"Sure." Lani wished she could fast-forward through Ms O'Connor's instructions; there were much more important matters on her mind than how she was going to carry her lunch tray. "I'm sure everyone will be fine with helping out." *For as long as I'm around, anyway,* she added silently.

"Good. You can stop by here every other day and I'll check on the bandage. Now I suggest you go back to your room and rest for a while. I'll give you something for the pain."

"Thank you, Ms O'Connor," Mrs Hernandez said. "We appreciate all you've done for Lani."

Lani glanced at her mother, whose voice sounded calm and pleasant as usual. She looked calm and pleasant, too, in her tasteful sky-blue trouser suit and chunky heels. Was she thinking about how professional and capable the staff was at Chestnut Hill, and therefore what a wonderful place it would be for Lani to stay? Somehow, Lani didn't think so…

"Let's roll, people." Commander Hernandez glanced at his watch. "We don't have much time before we're due in Dr Starling's office."

Lani's stomach flip-flopped. "I can still come with

you to the meeting, right? I swear I'll rest as soon as we're done."

"I'm sorry, cowgirl." Her father's eyes were sympathetic, but his voice was firm. "Your mother and I can handle the meeting. The most important thing for you to do is follow Nurse O'Connor's orders and get some rest."

That turned out to be a difficult order to obey. After her parents walked her back to her dorm room and left again, Lani peeled off her ripped and dirty riding clothes and pulled on sweats. The simple task of changing clothes took much longer than usual thanks to her injured wrist, and by the time she finished she found herself surprisingly worn out. She lay down on her bed, but her mind wouldn't stop racing. Had her parents reached Dr Starling's office yet? What were they saying? It was frustrating to imagine that the three adults might, at that very moment, be deciding Lani's future without her.

I didn't even have a chance to tell Dad about my new study schedule, she thought in despair. *Or explain about Rodeo Day. Or...*

"Ow!" Lani yelped as she shifted positions and banged her injured wrist against the mattress. Tears sprang to her eyes as she sat up and cradled her arm against her body until the pang subsided. Her wrist hurt, her heart hurt, and it didn't feel like things could possibly get any worse.

The dorm room felt very empty, and she wished her friends were there to keep her company while she waited to learn her fate. If anyone could help her feel a little better through something like this, it was the three of them.

Unfortunately, there wasn't much hope of them showing up anytime soon, as much as Lani was sure they wanted to be there to support her. It would probably be a good hour before they finished at the stable – after all, her fall had come less than halfway through the class, and the others would be expected to finish their ride after taking care of Colorado. Even when they finished, they would still have to untack their own ponies, sponge and walk them, wipe down their tack, and help around the barn. It made Lani heartstoppingly lonely to think of them doing those things without her that day... and even lonelier to imagine that soon they might be doing them without her all the time.

Don't give up! she told herself fiercely. *Maybe at this very moment, Dr Starling is convincing Dad and Mom to give Chestnut Hill another chance. Stranger things have happened.*

Giving up on trying to rest, she got up and did her best to occupy her mind with homework. But the next forty minutes crept past as slowly as a walk around the ring on Colorado on one of his rare lazy days, and at one point she realized she'd been staring at the same map in her geography textbook for a good fifteen minutes. Finally Lani heard a sharp rap on her door.

"Come in!" she called, jumping out of her desk chair so abruptly it sent another jolt through her aching arm.

Her parents walked in, shrugging off their winter coats. "How are you feeling?" her mother asked, slinging her shearling jacket onto Malory's neatly made bed and hurrying toward Lani. "Does your arm still hurt?"

"A little." Lani brushed aside the question with an impatient wriggle of her good hand. "Look, don't keep me in suspense. What happened in the meeting?"

She held her breath as her parents exchanged a glance.

"Sit down, Lani," her father said.

She sank onto the edge of her bed, staring at them. Her father leaned against her desk while Mrs Hernandez perched on Alexandra's desk chair. Their faces were very serious.

"We won't keep you in suspense, Lani," Commander Hernandez began. "We just had an interesting talk with Dr Starling. She shared a few things with us – including the detention your French teacher gave you for lateness."

Lani winced. "That wasn't a big deal, really," she said. "Mme. Dubois is kind of grumpy sometimes, and I was only late that day because I overslept after staying up studying really hard."

"Regardless." Her father rubbed his chin. "That, together with your fall today, seems to be telling us something. Namely, that our instincts were right – Chestnut Hill just isn't the place for you."

Even though she'd been expecting and dreading and bracing herself for this very moment for more than a week, Lani felt tears spring to her eyes. "You're wrong!"

she blurted out. "Chestnut Hill is perfect for me!"

"We're sorry, sweetie." Her mother's expression was sympathetic but unwavering. "We know you're having fun here. But we sent you here for an education, not just to have a great time."

Lani's father nodded. "Your priorities here clearly lie outside of your schoolwork. We thought that allowing you to attend a school with horseback riding would inspire you, but instead it seems to be distracting you. This fund-raising rodeo business your riding instructor was telling us about is just one more example of that."

"But that's different!" Lani blurted out. "Anyway, you should be proud of me – I'm, like, the only seventh-grader ever to be in charge of a fund-raising committee."

"It's nice that you're so devoted to riding and other activities," her mother said. "But we can't let that get in the way of your academics."

"But—" Lani began.

"But nothing," her father said briskly. "If your head wasn't so full of horses, maybe you'd be better able to meet your academic potential. You can't expect to get into a decent college with marks like the ones you brought home last term. Never mind med school!"

Lani winced, and this time it had nothing to do with her throbbing wrist. Her father seemed to assume she was aiming for a high-flying medical career, just like Dacil and Guadeloupe. She'd never bothered to try to convince him otherwise, or to tell him she'd always thought she might want to be a college professor or a research scientist instead. Or maybe something completely different than any of those things... Why did she have to figure this stuff out now, in seventh grade, anyway?

I know Dad has ambitions for all of us, she thought with a twinge of resentment, *but maybe I have different ambitions for myself. Did he ever think about that?*

She wanted to speak up, to use her famous powers of persuasion to convince them that they were wrong about her, that she could keep up with her riding and her friends and other extracurriculars and still study her butt off at the same time. Hadn't she been doing exactly that for the past couple of weeks?

Yeah, and look where that got me, she thought dismally, fingering a pulled thread on her bedspread with her good hand.

"Are you OK, Lani?" her father asked, clearly a bit surprised at her silence. "Do you want to say anything about this?"

"Yeah," she blurted out. "I – I – you don't understand. I've been studying really hard this term, and I'm sure my next report card will be better. Plus, the thing with the fund-raiser is, it's for a really good cause. See, there's a Chestnut Hill alum named Dr Jordan who started this foundation..."

She searched her mind for the impassioned, persuasive words she'd used at the fund-raising meeting. But this time, her mind failed her. It was easy for her to debate with friends, strangers, her sisters – most people, really. But her parents were different. She knew the most important thing to them was doing what they thought was best for her. If they really believed she would be better off at a different school, no amount of cajoling would make any difference.

Before she could go on, her father shook his head. "I'm truly sorry, Lani," he said. His voice was kind, yet beneath it lay a steely edge of determination. "We appreciate how much you wanted to have a chance to ride alongside studying, but it just hasn't worked out. I'm afraid we've made up our minds. After spring break, you'll be leaving Chestnut Hill."

Chapter Nine

Lani leaned on the rail of the jumping arena, watching gloomily as Lynsey rode Bluegrass over a tricky course. It was Friday, two days after Lani's crash, and the rest of her intermediate riding class was winding up that day's lesson. Even though Lani couldn't ride, she was allowed to watch the others. She hadn't bothered to change out of her school uniform, and the winter breeze raised goose bumps on her legs beneath her royal-blue kilt despite her grey tights.

"All right, that's it for today," Ms Carmichael called as Lynsey pulled up her pony. "You all did well that time, so let's end on a positive note. Please walk your horses for a few minutes to cool them down, then put them away."

As her friends started walking their ponies around the ring, Lani pushed herself away from the rail with her good arm and headed into the stable. She'd left her schoolbag there, and while she waited for the others to return, she pulled out her history textbook. She'd given up on her strenuous studying schedule after the disastrous meeting with her parents, but that didn't mean she was giving up on her schoolwork entirely. She wanted to make sure she entered her next school with decent marks. Sitting down on a handy bale of hay, she opened her book and started to read.

"There you are!" Dylan exclaimed, bursting into the barn a few minutes later with Morello trailing behind her. "Where'd you disappear to so fast?"

Lani shrugged. "It's chilly out there," she said. "No point standing out in the wind if I don't have to, right?"

"Sure, I guess." Dylan frowned. "Come on, Mo-mo," she said to the pony, who was eyeing Lani's hay bale chair hungrily. "Let's get you untacked and all snuggled up in your blanket, hmm?"

She continued down the aisle to the pony's stall. The rest of the class followed her, most of them chattering about the course they'd just jumped. Lynsey and Nadia led their ponies into their respective stalls, which were across the aisle from each other, and quickly removed their bridles. Then they disappeared through the far end of the barn, calling out something about returning to finish untacking after they got a drink of water.

Malory paused in front of Lani, allowing Tybalt to eyeball the book she was reading, which he seemed to think was some kind of pony-eating monster. "Did you see how well he did that last time through?" she gasped, her eyes shining with pride as she patted the bay gelding on the neck. "It was like he'd been doing it forever. Who knows, maybe we will be ready to tackle that cross-country course by the time it's done!"

Lani forced a smile. Malory completely deserved to be proud of Tybalt's progress. "He looked great, Mal. You've really come a long way with him."

"Did somebody mention the cross-country course?" Dylan popped back into view in the doorway of Morello's stall. "Because Morello and I are first in line. Unless Colorado the speedball barrel horse beats us there, of course." She raised her eyebrows at Lani.

Lani knew that her friends were trying to cheer her up, just as they'd been doing since Wednesday. They knew her parents' visit hadn't gone well – the trouble was, she hadn't told them exactly how not-well it had gone. She hadn't told them she was going to be leaving Chestnut Hill in a few short weeks. If she said it, it would only make it real. Instead, she'd let them believe that the whole decision was still up in the air – that if she studied extra hard, she might still change her parents' minds. That had the added bonus of giving her the perfect excuse to escape into her books whenever she started to feel overwhelmed by everything. It was a miserable feeling, purposely separating herself like that. But Lani reckoned it was something she had to do.

Honey had put Falcon in the cross-ties. The bay pony grew a heavy coat no matter how often he was clipped and thus required more extensive grooming than most of the others, and Honey was diligent about scraping him until every hair was dry.

"It's too bad you're missing these great jumping classes this week, Lani," she commented as she rubbed

Falcon's shoulder with a rag. "You and Colorado will have some catching up to do when you're back in the saddle."

"Yeah, I guess," Lani said. "It might be a while before I can really ride again, though." *Maybe much longer than any of you think.*

"What do you mean?" Dylan sounded surprised. "I thought Nurse O'Connor said two weeks."

"That's if everything heals properly." Lani shrugged, sending a fresh pang through her injured arm. "It might be longer. And my wrist still hurts a lot."

Her friends were silent. "Well," Malory said at last, "that's OK. It's not like anyone else in our class is riding Colorado in the meantime. At least you can still spend time with him."

Glancing down the aisle, Lani noticed for the first time that the buckskin pony was hanging his head out over his door. His eyes were half closed and he appeared to be dozing, but she still felt a flash of guilt for ignoring him. She made a move to stand up and go over to give him a scratch.

Then she stopped herself. *Why bother?* she thought hopelessly. *If I keep my distance from Colorado now, maybe it won't hurt quite as much when I have to say goodbye.*

Suddenly she realized that her friends were all staring at her, and Lani felt her face flush. She knew they could see she wasn't herself, and that they were waiting for her to tell them what was wrong. But she couldn't bring herself to tell them the truth. Not yet.

Maybe I need to start keeping my distance from them, too, she thought, lowering her gaze to her textbook to keep them from seeing the tears suddenly filling her eyes.

Lani managed to keep her friends at arm's length until the next day, Saturday. They were supposed to take the ten a.m. bus into Cheney Falls. It would be their first trip into town this term, and Dylan, Honey, and Malory had been full of excited plans all week. As much as they loved Chestnut Hill, it was nice to get away from the campus once in a while, far from schoolbooks and other responsibilities. During these weekend excursions into town, they could browse the stores at the mall, ice-skate at the public rink, hang out at the cinema or bowling alley, or grab some food at one of the local eateries.

Somehow, though, the thought of a day in Cheney Falls didn't feel like the grand expedition it usually did to Lani. In fact, it sounded downright painful. For the past day and a half, she'd been trying to work up the energy to tell her friends she didn't feel like going with them. But she hadn't pulled it off just yet.

"Ready?" Malory prompted, bouncing in from the bathroom and grabbing her coat from the back of her desk chair. She shrugged it on, then tucked her wallet in the back pocket of her well-worn Levi's. "We don't want to miss the bus, or we'll have to wait for the twelve-thirty and we'll be late meeting the guys. Can you believe Honey's finally having a real date with Josh? How cool is that?"

Lani glanced up from her bed, where she was reading her science textbook. With a flash of guilt, she realized she'd completely forgotten it was Honey's big day. She knew Malory was excited about seeing Caleb again, too – he was planning to meet them in town as well.

"Um, I think I need to skip the trip to town this week," she said, feeling guiltier than ever but trying to sound casual. "I just remembered I told Noel I could meet with her today to go over what we've been doing on the Activities Committee. Besides, my wrist still hurts, and I don't want to mess it up by bouncing around on that creaky old bus."

Neither part of her excuse was exactly true. In fact, her next meeting with Noel wasn't until that evening after dinner. And her wrist was feeling much better. But Lani thought that what her friends didn't know wouldn't hurt them, and being busy and injured had given her a great excuse to keep her distance from Colorado. That was why she still wore her sling most of the time, even though she didn't really need it.

Malory paused in the midst of zipping up her coat. "What? Are you sure?" she said. "But we said we'd all meet Nat and Caleb and Josh at the coffee shop. It just won't be as fun. Without you around, we might have to feign some serious conversation."

"Oh, the horror," Lani declared.

"See what I mean?"

"I know, I know, but I think you'll make out OK." Lani forced a cheerful smile, feeling horrible about letting Honey down. But what was the point of getting to know the Saint Kits boys any better if she was leaving at the end of the term? "I'm totally bummed to miss out on the big moment. You guys will have to tell me all about it the second you get back, OK? I'm sure you'll have an awesome time."

"But don't you think Noel could wait until later?" Malory said, peering closely into her face. "I'm sure she'd understand if you told her you already made plans..."

"I don't think so." Lani pushed her book away, then stood up and reached for her Converse high-tops. "We have a ton to do to get ready, and I just wouldn't feel right putting it off, you know? Work before fun and all that. Speaking of which, I'd better get moving, or I'll be late – I promised her I'd make some copies of our agenda before I meet with her, and you know how there's always a line at the Xerox machines on weekends..."

She continued babbling on cheerily in the same vein until she had her sneakers on and tied. Then she grabbed her jacket and headed for the door.

"But—" Malory began.

"See you later!" Lani called with as much peppiness as she could muster. "Have fun in town, OK?"

With that, she darted out the door and hurried down the hall toward the stairs. She kept up the brisk pace until she was safely outside and away from Adams, then slowed to a stroll.

Taking off her sling and jamming her hands into her

pockets, she stared at the ground, not interested in making eye contact with any of the other students walking past. She wasn't in the mood to talk to anybody – especially not her closest friends. The thought of squeezing into a booth in the noisy, overheated coffee shop, forcing herself to talk and laugh and tease her friends as if nothing had changed, was almost unbearable. Everything had changed; her friends just didn't know it yet.

With a start, Lani realized her feet had automatically taken her down the familiar path to the barn. There were no riding classes that day, and most of the ponies were turned out in the paddocks along the main drive. She could see Morello and Tybalt grazing on the winter-brown grass in one of them, but there was no sign of Colorado.

She entered the barn and almost immediately saw his familiar buckskin face looking out of his stall. "Hey, boy," she called to him. "What are you doing inside on a beautiful day like this?"

Kelly stuck her head out of the stall, startling Lani. "He just had his feet done," she explained cheerfully, pushing her long blonde hair out of her eyes. "The farrier had to come put Lucky's shoe back on, so while he was here I asked him to trim a few of the ponies that were looking long. I already turned out Bella and Flight, but I hadn't got around to him yet. Want to give me a hand? Is your wrist feeling up to it?"

"Sure," Lani said at once. "Where should I put him?"

"Tudor, Hardy, and Falcon are out in the triangle -

pasture," Kelly replied. "He can go in with them. Thanks, Lani!"

"No problem." With her good hand, she caught the lead rope Kelly tossed her. As the stable hand headed for the tack room, Lani gave Colorado a rub on his neck. "How's it going, boy?"

Colorado snuffled curiously at her jacket pockets, looking for treats. Lani grinned as he nosed her stomach. She pushed him away gently but firmly, not wanting to encourage any bad habits, even cute ones.

"Come on," she said, her grin wavering as she felt herself on the verge of tears again. How many more times would she share a moment like this with him? "I'm sure you don't want to stand around in here with me. Let's get you outside with your buddies."

She spent the next twenty minutes leaning on the paddock fences, watching the ponies standing in the watery sun. Colorado settled next to Falcon, the two ponies standing nose to tail so they could swish at the occasional fly that bothered them. Finally Lani realized that her fingers and toes were going numb, and her wrist was starting to ache for real. She shivered and turned away, reaching into her pocket for her sling. Then she headed toward the dorm, figuring it was safe to return by now. Her friends would have long since departed to catch the minivan to Cheney Falls.

But when she opened the door to her room, she found Malory, Dylan, and Honey sitting in an expectant row on her bed.

"Surprise," Dylan said dryly.

"What are you guys doing here?" Lani demanded, her stomach dropping. "I thought you were going into town."

"We were." Honey gazed at her, her kind blue eyes wide with concern. "We canceled because we were worried about you."

Malory smiled sympathetically. "We knew something must really be wrong if you were willing to pass up the chance to matchmake between Honey and Josh!"

"We didn't want you to miss out on the romance of the century," Dylan agreed. "So we called the boys and postponed the big date."

"But I told Mal," Lani protested. "I have a meeting with Noel. Otherwise I definitely would have—"

"Don't dig yourself in any deeper," Dylan said sternly. "We already know you were making that up."

"Yeah," Malory said with a shrug. "We ran into Noel in the line for the bus to Cheney Falls."

Honey nodded. "So we knew there had to be something you weren't telling us, and we came back to find out what it was."

"Oh." Lani stood in the doorway for a moment, feeling choked up. How come she had such amazing, caring, forgiving friends? "You guys," she began, her voice cracking. "You guys are—" She couldn't find the words, so she just shrugged.

"We know, we know," Dylan said. "We're amazing, incredible, unbelievable. But enough about us. What's up with you? We know you had a tough week, but you've been walking around like a zombie for the past few days. And now you're, like, lying to us and missing out on fun and stuff, which totally isn't like you. So what's the deal?"

Lani knew it was time to tell them the truth. Actually, it was *way past* time – she was already wondering why she hadn't told them everything in the first place.

"Fine, fine, fine," she said with mock exasperation. "If you guys are going to be so nosy, you can share my pain. Just remember, you asked for it!" Leaning against the edge of Malory's desk, she glanced around at them somberly. "When my parents were here the other day?..."

She filled them in on everything her parents had said after the meeting with Dr Starling. When she got to what her father had said about her leaving Chestnut Hill for good at spring break, Dylan let out a loud gasp.

"No way! How can your dad yank you out of here without even considering your opinion? Maybe you'd better let me talk to him..."

Despite her anxiety, Lani let out a short burst of laughter. The thought of impulsive, outspoken Dylan berating her father made for a pretty entertaining mental picture.

"Thanks," she said. "But I don't think it would do any good. Once Dad makes up his mind, it usually stays made up."

"But that's not fair," Malory protested.

"I know. I tried to talk to them already, believe me,

but they wouldn't listen. It's like they'd already decided they're right about this, and they're not going to think about it anymore."

Dylan was shaking her head. "No way," she said firmly. "You can't let them do this, Lani. There's only one answer – you'll have to get your marks back up to perfect, that's all. They're not taking you away until spring break, right? That's weeks away! Prove you can do it all – school, horses, the fund-raiser – with energy to spare. That way your parents will have no option but to let you stay, right? I mean, if you get a mid-term progress report full of A's and A-pluses, that's their whole argument shot to pieces!"

"I don't know," Lani began uncertainly. "It really seems like their minds are made up no matter what I do or say. I'm sure they're already in contact with my sisters' school. Why burn myself out for nothing?"

"You can't think that way!" Dylan retorted. "All we need is a plan of attack."

Lani shrugged, but she also felt a tiny spark of hope. Dylan was just about the only person she knew who was as stubborn as her father. Could she be right about this?

"What's the plan?" Honey asked.

Dylan stood up and started pacing between Lani's bed and the window. "We need to tackle this on a subject-by-subject basis," she said. "Honey, you're amazing at English and French. How about if you tutor her in those?"

"I'd be glad to," Honey answered instantly. "I mean, *oui, oui*!"

Getting into her stride, Dylan whirled around and jabbed one finger toward Malory. "Mal, you and I can help out with history and geography. We both do pretty well in those. That only leaves maths and science."

"I can handle those myself," Lani spoke up, feeling enthusiasm and energy bubble up inside her for the first time in days. "If I can't ace those subjects, I don't deserve to stay."

"That's the spirit!" Dylan exclaimed. "This isn't only about marks, though. We all know you can pull that off. But you could get good marks anywhere. You also have to show your parents why Chestnut Hill is special for reasons way beyond marks."

"The fund-raiser," Honey said, as if reading her mind.

Dylan nodded. "Exactly. If Lani keeps her marks up while helping organize the best darn fund-raiser the state of Virginia has ever seen, even a stubborn old coot like Commander Hernandez has to sit up and take notice." She shot Lani a slightly sheepish glance. "Um, no offence to your dad."

"None taken." Lani grinned. Maybe she *had* been too quick to give up. After all, hadn't Marta said the same thing her friends were saying now? Yes, their father was stubborn and hardheaded, but he was impressed when people showed equal amounts of persistence. If she could prove herself in all these areas, her parents would have to give her some credit – and maybe even reconsider their decision.

All we can do is try, she told herself as her friends

started discussing their plans in more detail, *because the only thing worse than having to leave Chestnut Hill would be leaving without knowing I'd done everything I possibly could to stay.*

"And I really think the whole event will come off much more professionally if we hire someone to be the MC," Lynsey insisted. "I'm sure my mother can find us somebody good who'll work for a reasonable fee, considering this is for charity."

"Yeah," Patience put in. "Lynsey's mom knows lots of celebrities."

"Really? You think she could get us a celebrity?" Tanisha Appleton asked with interest. "Like who?"

"Oh, I don't know. Somebody good, I'm sure." Lynsey waved one hand airily, then turned and stared at Lani. "So how about it?"

Lani sighed, picking at the nubby fabric arm of the sofa in the underclassmen's lounge. It was Wednesday, and she was running a meeting of the Activities Committee for the Rodeo Day fund-raiser. The meeting had been going on for more than an hour, and she couldn't stop feeling guilty about all the homework waiting for her back in her room. She'd spent the past three and a half days trying to maintain her optimism about Dylan's plan. But it wasn't easy, especially with Lynsey and Patience, who weren't even technically on her -committee, buzzing in her ear all the time and making things more difficult – more extravagant – than they had to be.

At this rate, how am I going to make it to spring break? Lani wondered wearily. Then another thought popped into her head uninvited: *What if Dad is right? Maybe Chestnut Hill is too much for me. Maybe I need to drop all this fund-raiser business, let someone else take over, and focus on my schoolwork...*

"Lani!" Lynsey's voice grew more strident. "Are you even listening to me?"

"Whatever, Lynsey," Lani snapped. "I'm tired of arguing about this. If you're so convinced about this stupid professional MC thing, let's do it your way. Then maybe you'll go back to the Food Committee and leave us alone to get some work done."

Lynsey smirked. "I'm glad you understand I have more experience in this arena than you do, Lani. Now if you'll excuse me, I have a phone call to make."

She flounced out of the room with Patience following her like an adoring puppy as usual.

Dylan rounded on Lani, her eyes wide with astonishment. "Are you out of your mind?" she demanded. "Why'd you cave like that? You know it'll be way more fun to have students and faculty do the MC-ing."

Lani shrugged. "What difference does it make? We have more important issues to worry about. It's not like anyone will even notice who's MC-ing one way or the other."

"*I'll* notice," Dylan retorted. "Especially every time I look over and see Miss Snooty McSmuggypants and her number one fan, Patience Duvall, congratulating themselves on whatever pretty-boy C-list celeb Mrs Harrison digs up for us."

At the sound of raised voices, the faculty adviser, assistant housemother, Jacqueline Sebastian, glanced up from the papers she was reading. "I'm sure it will work out fine," she said soothingly.

Honey nodded. "Right," she said. "Should we talk about the schedule of events now?"

Dylan seemed happy enough to stop complaining about Lynsey and Patience and join Honey and the other committee members in discussing the event's ever–evolving schedule. The goal of the meeting was to come up with a full, updated Rodeo agenda before the joint committee meeting later that evening in the upperclass lounge, and that meant the Activities Committee had a lot of ground to cover.

But as the others talked excitedly about possible schedules, Lani's mind drifted. It had been exactly one week since her riding accident. Her wrist still ached a little, although not enough to justify wearing her sling as regularly as she was doing. But that was the least of her probleMs Dylan's plan for Lani to prove herself to her parents was in full swing – Lani's friends were tutoring her every day at lunch and in the evenings, and several of her teachers had already complimented her work and her dedication to her extra-credit projects. The others seemed to think their plan was guaranteed to work, but now that her initial rush of optimism had passed, Lani wasn't so sure. She was already feeling exhausted, even though she wasn't riding yet. How would she ever fit Colorado into her new schedule? What was the point of staying at Chestnut Hill if all she ever did was study?

The others just don't know what my family's like, Lani thought, staring down at the toes of her favourite cowboy boots and feeling a little sorry for herself. *They don't understand how it is for me, having to prove myself around three brilliant older sisters and a couple of super-successful parents...*

"Lani? Have you been listening to anything we've said in the last fifteen minutes?"

Lani snapped back to attention. "Sorry, Dyl, I was just thinking about – about something," she stammered. "What were you saying?"

Dylan frowned. "Could I talk to you for a minute?" she said. "Excuse us, guys."

She stomped off to a corner of the room. Lani gave the others an apologetic shrug. "I'll be right back," she said.

"Sure," eleventh-grader Rosie Williams said, shooting Dylan a curious glance. "No problem."

When Lani joined Dylan in the corner, she could see that her friend was fuming. "What's wrong?" she asked.

"What's wrong?" Dylan shot back. "I was just going to ask you the same question! I mean, should we reschedule this meeting for sometime when you're paying attention?" she asked sarcastically. "What with letting Lynsey do whatever she wants and spacing out when we're trying to work out the schedule, I'm starting to think you don't really want to be here."

"Well, excuse me!" Lani snapped back. She was suddenly fed up with pretending to be super-organized when it felt like her entire world was falling apart. "I happen to have a few things on my mind right now, OK? So sue me if I'm not hanging on your every brilliant word."

"Guys—" Honey called from the other end of the room, sounding nervous. "Everything OK over there?"

Before the mood could deteriorate any further, the door swung open with a bang. Malory stood there, panting and red-faced with her curly dark hair flying wildly in all directions.

"You'll never believe this!" she cried. "I just ran into Theresa Rahman – she's on the Food and Hospitality Committee, you know. She told me she just found out the caterer we all liked is out – someone called them and canceled the whole event!"

Chapter Ten

"What?" Lani was on her feet almost before the words were out of Malory's mouth. "What are you talking about? They were the only ones who would do barbecue. There must be some mistake – I talked to Rachel Goodhart just last night, and she said everything was cool with the catering deal! And she's the head of the committee, so she should know the score."

"I know." Malory leaned over and rested her hands on her knees, still trying to catch her breath. "That's what I told Theresa. But she called the caterer an hour or so ago to confirm the date or something, and they told her a girl from Chestnut Hill called first thing this morning to say we'd changed our minds and wouldn't need them after all."

"Who has a phone?" Lani demanded. Several options were immediately pulled out of pockets and offered. She picked Tanisha's brand-new Palm Treo and dialed Rachel Goodhart's mobile number, which was printed on the list of committee heads tucked into her notebook. Then she hurried off to a quiet corner so she could hear clearly.

A few minutes later, she hung up and rejoined the group, feeling nothing but relief.

"Well?" Honey prompted.

"Rachel heard about this from Theresa, too, and she was already taking care of it. She knew we needed that caterer. We're back on their schedule, and they'll be here for Rodeo Day as planned," Lani reported. "Luckily, they hadn't given away our date yet."

"So what happened?" Malory asked. She had flopped on one of the upholstered chairs, her shoes off and her feet up on an ottoman.

"Patience," Lani replied grimly.

Dylan's eyes narrowed. "No way!"

"Yes way," Lani said. "Rachel sounded pretty mad about it, too."

Wei Lin Chang, who was one of Patience's roommates, wrinkled her nose in confusion. "But why would Patience cancel the caterer?"

"Since when does Patience need a reason to do obnoxious things?" Dylan said. "She's probably just trying to cause trouble. As usual."

The others, including Wei Lin, nodded ruefully. Everyone in Adams knew about the time Patience had ratted on Dylan when she'd gone down to the barn after curfew.

Honey gasped. "Wait! I just remembered," she cried. "Yesterday morning at breakfast, I passed by Patience's table and noticed she was looking at some flyers from some fancy-looking catering service. I thought it was sort of odd at the time. But I assumed her dad was planning a party to launch his latest book or something like that."

"That explains everything," Lani said. "Patience probably thought this was a good way to suck up to Lynsey – you know, get rid of the caterer we picked so she can use the hoity-toity one Lynsey suggested in the first place."

Dylan pursed her lips grimly. "Sounds like Lynsey's plan must've been shot down in their committee meeting. At least that means the food committee wants to make this a fun, western event – not some froufrou cocktail napkin affair," she said.

Honey grimaced. "You're right," she said. "Now we know that everyone's on board. Everything will be authentic!"

Lani accessed Tanisha's address book on the cell phone and pressed dial when she found the number she was looking for.

"Who are you calling now?" Malory asked.

"Lynsey," Lani replied, putting the phone to her ear. She could feel herself positively fizzing with energy, electricity sparking through her fingers and toes. The close call with the caterer had reminded her of what was really important in the few weeks she had left at Chestnut Hill, which was doing her part to put together a great event for the benefit of those AllSports kids. She could go back to feeling sorry for herself later. For now, she had work to do. "I'm going to tell her to scratch the professional MC," she added. "I've just made an executive decision – we're sticking with the original plan to play that part ourselves."

Dylan grinned. "Welcome back, Lani!"

from: Mherndz04
to: ponygurllani
subject: re: Rodeo Day

Hi Lani,

It sounds like your fund-raiser is going full steam ahead! Congrats, I know how much work it can be to put together something like that. I'm glad you're not giving up on having a good time at CH, no matter how things turn out at the end of the year.

Anyway, I had a great idea – why don't you contact Belle Carter and see if she wants to come to your event? She's always doing charity stuff; it's probably right up her alley! And how could she resist helping a young Colorado Springs neighbour like you?

Keep me posted on the plans! If I can swing it, I may fly down there for the weekend to cheer you on!
M.

Lani skimmed her sister's email again, feeling dubious. Belle Carter was a nationally famous barrel racer who was based just outside Colorado Springs. Lani had seen her run several times at the Colorado

State Fair in nearby Pueblo, and the Rooftop Rodeo in the northern part of the state. At just twenty-five years old, Belle had already been at the top of the money-earner charts for more than two years. She was also a popular celebrity in Colorado, appearing on TV and at local events, and endorsing various equestrian products.

"Yeah, right," Lani murmured under her breath. "Like she'd really fly all the way out here to Virginia just because I asked her to."

Just get it done, cowgirl. Her father's words floated through her head.

With a shrug, she decided to do just that. Why not go ahead and ask? The worst Belle Carter could do was say no.

Lani Googled Belle's name and soon came up with the website for her ranch. There was a contact email, and Lani quickly typed up a note describing the Rodeo Day event, giving the date and explaining that all the money raised would be going to AllSports. She hit send without much hope of getting a response. What were the chances that a genuine celebrity like Belle Carter would care about some amateur school fund-raiser? She was probably too busy to check her email, let alone take time out of her schedule for Chestnut Hill's Rodeo Day.

Telling herself that at least she'd tried, Lani clicked onto Chestnut Hill's website. Carrie Janes, a ninth-grader who was something of a computer genius, had created a link from the main site to a special page about the Rodeo Day fund-raiser. Lani had called Carrie an hour ago, right after that afternoon's committee meeting, and Carrie had promised to add the latest information right away so it would be available before the general meeting that night.

Lani found the link to the Rodeo Day page and couldn't resist a broad grin when she saw that Carrie had done just as she'd promised. The fund-raiser page looked fantastic! Carrie had created a big headline using Western-looking rope type, and below that she'd inserted several images of Western riders performing different moves. The new information was in place, along with all the other details the various committees had worked out so far.

Realizing that she should have included a link to the site in her message to Belle Carter, Lani switched back to her email. To her surprise, there was a new message in her inbox.

"Wow, that was fast," she murmured, her heart sinking as she noted Belle Carter's return address on the email. "Guess she wanted to let me down easy right away."

She clicked it open.

from: CARTERRANCH01
to: ponygurllani
subject: re: Chestnut Hill School Rodeo Day

Dear Ms Hernandez,

I happened to be sitting in the ranch office when your email came in, and I wanted to write back personally right away. You may not know it, but my younger sister has a learning disability, so I know all about the good work that AllSports is doing. She learned to play tennis with a similar group a year or two ago. It would be a thrill and an honor to help your school raise money for the group. And as it happens, I'm doing a series of clinics on the East Coast starting at the end of this week, so I'll be in your neck of the woods, anyway...

There was more, but Lani was hardly able to take it in. All she could do was stare at the sign-off at the bottom of the message: *See you soon, Belle Carter.*

"Whoo-hoo!" she yelled, leaping out of her chair.

"What?" Malory yelped. She was sitting at one of the other computers, typing up the agenda for that evening's meeting. "What's wrong?"

Lani grinned at her. "Nothing," she declared. "Absolutely nothing. You're not going to believe this, but Belle Carter wants to take part in our Rodeo Day!"

"Who?"

"Belle Carter." Lani tried to be patient, reminding herself that most of her friends at Chestnut Hill didn't follow Western disciplines. "She's only one of the most famous barrel racers in the whole entire country! I just wrote to her to tell her what we're doing, and she's willing to get involved!"

"Really?" Malory started to look excited, too. "That's awesome! What did she say?"

The two of them bent over the computer screen,

reading through the email. In the latter part of the note, Belle promised to bring one of her experienced barrel horses to do a demonstration.

"Check it out!" Lani pointed to a paragraph halfway through the email. "If anyone gets within three seconds of her time, she'll match the total funds raised for the whole day out of her own pocket! That's amazing! It'll be tough, though – a pro barrel racer can really lay down a fast—"

"Who's Chuck?" Malory interrupted, indicating something a little farther down the screen. "She says he might tag along. Is that one of her horses?"

Lani gasped. "No way! Does she really say that? I didn't even notice. Chuck isn't a horse – he's her boyfriend, Chuck Braxton. He rodeos, too – he mostly does roping and he used to ride bulls." She hit print to print out Belle's email, then opened a new email document.

"Are you writing back to Belle Carter right now?" Malory asked. "What are you going to say?"

Lani shook her head. "I'll do that in a minute," she said. "I should talk to Noel first – I guess we'll probably need to check with Dr Starling to make sure she's OK with having Belle and Chuck visit." She grinned. "Right now, I just need to email my sister and tell her she's a genius!"

One week later, the fund-raiser had gained so much momentum that Lani felt she was at the controls of a runaway train. Belle Carter's plans were confirmed –

she and Chuck Braxton had a clinic in Tennessee on Friday evening, so they were driving up to Chestnut Hill on Saturday morning with a couple of their horses. The entire school was abuzz with talk of the barrel-racing challenge. All the riding classes were practising around the school's new barrel course, which Ms Carmichael had agreed to leave set up in the outdoor ring until the big day.

Lynsey and a few of her hangers-on grumbled about turning the school into some kind of Hicksville Hoedown, but everyone else appreciated the chance to practise in hopes of posting the fastest time on Rodeo Day. In addition to the honour of winning the extra cash windfall for the charity, the housemothers had come up with an extra incentive – whichever rider met Belle's challenge got to choose the movie for the next Drive-In Movie Night. Of course, that was assuming that a Chestnut Hill girl was the one to win. That wasn't necessarily a given anymore, since at Noel's suggestion, Dr Starling had agreed to open the event to outsiders. Ever since, the members of the Publicity Committee had been fielding tons of calls from locals as well as nearby boarding schools. Lani and her friends had already received messages from their friends at Saint Kits, promising they'd be there.

All in all, the fund-raiser was reaching epic proportions. That meant Lani was kept busy almost nonstop. Between running committee meetings, meeting with Noel and the other committee heads, organizing every detail of the big day's activity schedule, and keeping up with her schoolwork, she was almost relieved not to have to worry about finding time to ride on top of everything else. It even helped her feel less guilty about avoiding Colorado. She missed him like crazy, but she figured it was better to get used to that feeling now, in case her plan to change her parents' minds didn't work.

Even if it does work, she reminded herself almost every time she walked past the path to the stables, *I might have to compromise – stay here at Chestnut Hill, but give up the riding programme. Maybe I should see my accident as a wake-up call. Because when it comes down to it, I guess I can give up riding if it means not having to give up my friends.*

If she brought her marks up, finished all her extra-credit projects, and pulled off this fund-raiser at the same time, her parents would see that she had what it takes to stay at Chestnut Hill. And if she gave up riding as well, they would know for sure that she was willing to compromise to get what she wanted.

If all goes well and they agree to let me stay, I can work even harder next year, she told herself. *And maybe after a term or two, they'll let me try the riding programme again...*

She was sure she could do it if she had to, but the very idea seemed almost too painful to contemplate. She didn't even want to mention it to her friends. That was the main reason she continued wearing her sling, even though her wrist was almost completely back to normal. Between her injury and her crazy schedule, she managed to avoid the whole topic of when she would start riding again.

She allowed herself a rare moment of relaxation as she sat on an upturned water bucket in the barn aisle and watched her friends tack up for their Wednesday afternoon riding class. One of the details she'd worked out over the past week, with the help of Alessandra di Schiapari of the Publicity Committee, was contacting a local English-Western tack shop and convincing them to loan the school several used Western saddles in exchange for displaying an advertising banner outside the main ring on the big day. Thanks to their efforts, almost a dozen borrowed saddles sat in the already crowded main tack room on temporary racks made of sawhorses. Matching Western headstalls shared hooks with the regular English bridles. Everyone in Lani's intermediate class except Lynsey had jumped at the chance to practise in the borrowed tack, and most lessons now included a half hour of optional practise of Western skills.

However, while most of them had caught on quickly to riding in a Western saddle, not everyone was as proficient yet in putting on the different tack. Lani grinned as she watched Honey struggle to tie her cinch. She'd put Falcon in the cross-ties, and the pony stood patiently as she fiddled with the unfamiliar rigging. As she poked at his side, trying to jam the strap behind the ring, he snorted and swung his quarters sideways.

"Hold still, Falcon," Honey begged as the end of the strap slipped out of her fingers for the third or fourth time. "Please! I've almost got it now."

Lani's grin widened. "Here, let me show you." She stood and hurried over to her friend. "You've got to leave the main part of the strap a little bit loose at first – that makes it easier to thread the end around behind the ring. See? Then when you have it knotted, you can tighten it down below like this." She demonstrated, smoothly tying and tightening Falcon's cinch.

"Oh! Cheers, Lani," Honey said with relief. "I knew I had to be doing something wrong." Her gaze fell on Lani's sling, which had slipped out of place as she pulled the cinch tight. "I hope doing that didn't hurt your wrist. How's it feeling today, anyway? Any better?"

"Oh – um, maybe a little. Still kind of sore, though."

"Hey!" Dylan exclaimed, hurrying toward them. "That reminds me – it's the two-week anniversary of when you fell and hurt your wrist, Lani. Are you sure it's still too sore to ride today? Colorado's in his stall – I'm sure Ms Carmichael would let you hop on if you remind her Nurse O'Connor said you only needed to rest for two weeks." She glanced down the aisle to where Malory was cursing softly under her breath as she tried to untangle the curb chain on her Western headstall. "And even though you'd be starting late, I bet you'd have him tacked up before the rest of us Eastern yahoos are even close to ready."

Lani smiled uncertainly. "I don't think that's such a good idea," she hedged. "Ms O'Connor said it would be *at least* two weeks, remember – I guess it's taking a little longer than she thought to heal."

"Oh." Dylan looked disappointed. "Bummer."

Honey shot Lani a sympathetic look. "You're smart to keep resting it if it's still bothering you," she said. "Better safe than sorry."

"Er, right." Lani felt a pang of guilt as the two girls returned to their horses. She hated fibbing to them, but she didn't know what else to do. *I'm still not sure they'll understand why I might have to give up riding,* she thought. *I'll have to figure out a way to explain it to them*… after *Rodeo Day*.

"You guys go ahead," she said as the others finished tacking up and got ready to lead their mounts out to the ring. "Tell Ms Carmichael I'll be there in a minute. I just want to check on Colorado."

When she was alone in the barn, she walked over to the buckskin gelding's stall. He was standing at the door munching on a mouthful of timothy.

"Hey, buddy," she said softly, reaching out to scratch him in his favorite spot. "Do you miss me? Because I sure miss you."

To her dismay, her eyes filled with tears. To avoid being seen by anyone, she unlatched his door and stepped inside to give him a hug. They just stood there for a few minutes, the pony snuffling at her hair as Lani tried to stop herself from breaking down altogether. Right at that moment, it didn't seem remotely fair that she might have to give up riding her favourite pony for ever.

Better that than going away to some school in California and never even seeing him again, she reminded herself sternly. *At least if I'm still here I can visit him and feed him carrots and maybe groom him once in a while. That's better than nothing.*

Pulling back, she gave the pony a pat on the neck and then wiped her tears with her jacket sleeve. Her gaze fell on his water bucket, which was almost empty.

"Looks like you were thirsty today, huh?" she said, pushing back her sling and reaching for the bucket. "Let me get you a refill before I head out to the ring."

She let herself out of the stall and hurried down the aisle to fill the bucket at one of the frost-free water hydrants. It felt nice to take care of the simple stable chore, and Lani did her best to savor the feeling… just in case she didn't get many more chances.

Chapter Eleven

"See you, Josh," Honey said shyly.

"Uh, see you, Honey," Josh replied, pushing his hand awkwardly through his floppy brown hair.

Lani grinned at Malory and Dylan. They grinned back. "Another successful end to another successful date," Dylan whispered.

"You girls coming, or are you going to spend the night here?" the bus driver called out.

"We're coming, we're coming," Dylan said. "Come on, Honey – our coach is about to turn into a pumpkin."

Honey was still blushing as she climbed onto the shuttle with the others. Lani was glad she'd been there to witness the first date with Josh after all. *I might as well enjoy this sort of stuff while I still can,* she reminded herself with a flash of familiar gloom.

But this time the feeling didn't last long. It had been too good a day.

"So how much money did you guys collect?" she demanded, settling in the seat beside Malory as the bus pulled on to the main street through Cheney Falls.

"Tons," Dylan replied, giving her collection can a satisfied shake. "Sold about a billion tickets, too."

Malory had turned to wave to the boys out the window, but now she looked over at her friends. "It was a good idea to come," she said. With a sly glance at Dylan, she added, "even if it was Lynsey's idea in the first place."

Lani nodded, shooting a quick look toward the back of the bus, where Lynsey and Patience were sitting. She'd been as surprised as anyone when Lynsey had come up with the plan to spend the Saturday before Rodeo Day in Cheney Falls dressed up as cowgirls, rattling collection cans, getting sponsorship, and selling tickets to the big event.

"I couldn't believe it at first," Dylan admitted, as if she had read Lani's mind. "But when I saw her show up at the bus stop this morning with her brand-new fringed suede Lulu Guinness handbag, everything suddenly became clear."

Malory laughed. "Yeah. Since when does carrying one little Western-type purse and wearing jeans count as 'dressing up like a cowgirl'?" she said, glancing down at her own outfit of blue jeans and a colourful tartan shirt.

Lani noticed that Honey was staring out the window, not taking part in the conversation at all. "Hey," she said, elbowing Dylan. "Check out Little Miss Daydream there. Think the date went well?"

Dylan grinned. "I don't know," she said. "Let's ask her. Oh, Honey..."

Honey turned to face them, blushing more deeply than ever. "Stop it," she said weakly. "You were there right along with me, so there's really nothing to tell."

"We weren't there just now," Malory pointed out with a mischievous grin. "When the two of you were getting so cosy all alone together outside the bus."

Honey shrugged. "We were just saying goodbye, that's all," she said. "No big deal."

Dylan cracked her knuckles. "I'm losing patience, so you'd better start talking, girl," she said. "Or would you rather have me tickle it out of you?"

"No!" Honey shrieked as Dylan reached toward her. "No tickling – please! I'll talk, I'll talk."

"Good." Lani laughed. "Let's hear it. What did he say to you? Did he tell you you're the most beautiful, charming girl in the universe, or what?"

"Well, not exactly." Honey looked bashful. "But he – he asked me out," she said. "Like, on a real date. To see a film."

"Shut up!" Dylan shrieked with joy. "Are you serious?"

Lani and Honey traded a grin. "Definitely a good day," Lani announced, deciding to take it as an omen of more good things to come. "Definitely!"

One hectic, frantic, surely-less-than-seven-days-long week later, Lani was out of bed and dressed well before her alarm went off at six a.m. Rodeo Day was here! As soon as she stepped out of the dorm, she could tell things were off to a good start – the tangy, inviting smell of barbecue was already floating through the chilly early morning air.

That must mean the caterers are here right on schedule – no last-minute Patience problems, Lani thought, recalling how Patience had tried to sabotage the event in the early stages of planning. But that incident seemed very far in the past by now – Patience had offered a grudging apology to the rest of the Food Committee, Lynsey had stopped pestering Lani's committee after learning there would be no celebrity MC after all, and that had been the end of it. In any case, Lani had more interesting things to think about than her snooty dorm mates. Taking a deep breath of the crisp, hickory-scented breeze, she stepped onto the path toward the barn. Just because she wasn't riding didn't mean she didn't have a million things to sort out before the day officially started at nine a.m. sharp!

Several hours later, the rest of the school was awake and the Rodeo Day was well under way. Crowds of visitors from outside the school had been pouring in ever since the gates opened at nine, and Lani was pretty sure everybody in the school was there as well. A half-dozen Adams girls were giving pony rides in the main ring, which was proving very popular; three of the quietest school horses were tacked up in Western saddles, while the leaders were outfitted in full cowgirl regalia, so everyone had a chance to take part in the rodeo experience. Local kids and even some non-riding Chestnut Hill students and teachers were lined up waiting to take their turn. Elsewhere, people were flocking to the food stands and vendor tables, bidding on cowboy-themed items at the silent auction, sampling the entries for the chili cook-off, or whooping and hollering as they tossed darts at cow-printed water balloons, shot fake rifles at the Ol' Saloon Shootin' Alley, or sampled a variety of other Western-themed carnival games.

Lani barely had time to throw a couple of darts and taste the hand-squeezed lemonade in between doing her part to take care of all the tiny background details that would make the event run smoothly. She was even busier than she'd been over the past couple of weeks, but for once she didn't mind. It was fun to rush around doing a little of this and a little of that, talking to her committee members and the other committee heads, and seeing how well everything was coming together. It made all the planning and all the meetings and the late nights seem totally worthwhile.

"Yo, Lani! Come here!" Dylan called as Lani rushed by in search of a glass of water for the auctioneer, a senior who was afraid her voice was about to give out halfway through the list of items up for sale.

Lani stopped and turned to see what her friend was doing. Dylan was standing beside the long, red-and-white tableclothed chili table slurping down a bowl of steaming chili from a Styrofoam cup. A girl Lani didn't know, but vaguely recognized as a Granville upperclassman, was just replacing the lid on the vat at one end. Several of the Food Committee members were mixing or serving out of other vats –

there were at least a dozen different chilis on the table, proving that the cook-off had been popular with a lot of senior students who had access to their own kitchen facilities.

"Is that one of the entries for the contest?" Lani asked.

Dylan nodded, her tongue darting out to lick a dab of tomato sauce off her lip. "You've got to taste this stuff!" she exclaimed. "I don't want to exaggerate, but this has got to be the most delicious chili in the entire history of the world!"

Lani grinned at the Granville upperclassman, who was beaming. "Sounds like you have your first vote right there."

"I hope so," the girl said. "I stayed up all night chopping up ingredients. It's my grandfather's recipe – he brought it with him from Montana."

Dylan held out a spoon dripping with chili. "Want a taste?"

Lani slurped it up. "Wow!" she exclaimed. "That *is* good. Almost as good as the chili back home in Colorado." She smirked at Dylan as the Granville girl pretended to scowl. "By the way, where's everybody else?" she asked.

Dylan swallowed another mouthful of chili. "Malory's checking on Tybalt – I think she's afraid he might spontaneously combust with all the excitement." She waved her plastic spoon at the crowds around them. "I think Honey volunteered to meet Dr Jordan and the group of kids she brought along. She was going to help them to their seats around the ring." She stirred her chili. "Has your sister shown up?"

"Not yet." Lani felt a pang of worry as she checked her watch. Marta had sent an email three days ago, promising to fly in for Rodeo Day, but there was no sign of her so far. Lani couldn't wait to show her sister how well the event had turned out. "I wish I had a mobile so she could call me whenever she finally gets here. I just hope her plane wasn't delayed."

"I'm sure she'll be here soon," Dylan said. "Who'd want to miss this?"

Lani grinned. Before she could say another word, she saw Honey rushing toward them. She skidded to a stop in front of Lani.

"They're here!" she blurted out.

Lani didn't even have to ask who she meant. "I'm on it," she said. "Are they in the main parking area?"

At Honey's nod, she took off at a jog. After a few steps, she paused and turned around. "Hey, you guys," she called back to her friends. "Can you take a glass of water to the auction stand for me?"

"Consider it done!" Dylan called back.

Lani smiled. "Thanks."

She spun on her heel and hurried off again, arriving in the parking lot just in time to see a gleaming silver horse trailer back into a spot marked off with a sign that read reserved for carter ranch. A moment later the rig's rumbling diesel engine cut off and two people jumped out of the cab. Lani recognized Belle Carter and Chuck Braxton right away. Belle, who was clad in snug-fitting Wranglers and a shearling-lined vest over her floral-print Western shirt, looked surprisingly petite and pretty up close – Lani was used to seeing her astride one of her horses, sweaty and red-faced after a hard run. Chuck looked as handsome and rugged as he always did in his jeans and Carhartt jacket, and for a moment Lani felt a little tongue-tied.

The moment passed. "Hi, you two!" she called, hurrying forward. "Welcome to Chestnut Hill!"

Belle turned to greet her with a smile. "Let me guess – you must be my neighbour, Lani Hernandez."

"That's right." Lani grinned and pumped her fist. "Colorado cowgirls rule!"

Belle and Chuck both laughed heartily. Once they'd finished trading introductions, Lani stood back and watched as the couple prepared to unload their horses. She couldn't help feeling a bit awed by being in the presence of two such well-known riders on the rodeo circuit, though the couple's friendly manners helped put her at ease. Belle explained that they'd left most of their string back in Tennessee where they were staying, bringing only one mount for each of them.

When Belle led the first horse down the ramp, Lani's eyes widened. "Hey, isn't that Ash?" she exclaimed, recognizing the famous American Quarter Horse gelding's distinctive dapple-grey coat and dark mane and tail.

Belle nodded, looking pleased. "Yes, it is," she said, giving the horse a fond pat. "He's the most experienced horse I brought east with me, so I thought he'd be the best choice to bring along today."

"Awesome!" Lani said appreciatively. "I saw you win on him at the last state fair back home. Of course, having the awesome Ash here is going to make it way harder for anyone to catch your time!"

Chuck grinned as he followed his girlfriend down the ramp, leading a stocky chestnut with three white socks. "You don't expect her to just give that money away, do you?"

"No way," Lani agreed, returning his grin. "What would be the fun of that?" She felt a moment of wistfulness at the thought of how her schoolmates would soon be galloping their ponies around those barrels, trying to match Belle's time. Glancing down at the sling she still wore on her arm, she couldn't help wondering what it would be like to join them.

But she pushed the thought away as quickly as it came. "Come on," she said to Belle and Chuck. "I'll show you the stalls we set up for your horses. You can let them rest up until it's time for you to ride."

"It's almost noon," Noel called out, hurrying toward the main food tent, where Lani was wolfing down a burger. "Are our special guests ready to do their exhibition?"

"I'll go check." Lani shoved the last bite of her food into her mouth as she headed toward the barn.

Inside, she found Ash and Chuck's chestnut, Doc, munching hay in their temporary stalls. Chuck was polishing the silver on his Western saddle with a rag, while Belle unloaded a set of protective bell boots from a bag. They both looked up when Lani skidded to a stop in front of them.

"Hey there," Chuck greeted her easily. "I'm guessin' from your face that we should be fixin' to saddle up soon, huh?"

"You guessed right," Lani replied. "We're ready whenever you guys are."

"It'll only take us a sec to tack up," Belle promised, already hurrying toward her horse's stall.

"Great," Lani said. "I'll go out and get ready to announce you."

Chuck winked at her. "Make sure you make us sound good, OK?"

Lani grinned, feeling tongue-tied once again. *That's the one problem with an all-girls' school*, she thought as she headed back outside. *You don't see guys like Chuck Braxton nearly often enough!*

Soon she was sitting in the announcer's area preparing to introduce Belle and Chuck. Noel and a couple of the other seniors had been taking turns announcing the other events and activities, but they had insisted that Lani do the honours for the riding exhibition. "After all," as Noel had said, "you're the reason those two are here."

Lani gave a look around. Across the ring she could see Dr Jordan surrounded by a small crowd of kids, who looked between seven and ten years old. They were all laughing and looking around. Lani noticed two girls at the end of a row who were holding hands. At that moment, Lani was so proud to be a part of the event that she didn't care how much money they raised. She knew it was about more than that.

"Ladies and gentlemen," Lani said into the microphone. She paused, amused by the sound of her own voice amplified and echoing over the crowded stable area. Then she continued. "Ladies and gentlemen, we have a fantastic Rodeo Day treat for you. Some special guests have come here all the way from Colorado Springs to show you what Western riding is all about."

She glanced toward the barn. Belle and Chuck had just led their horses outside. They started adjusting their fenders and preparing to mount. Figuring she had another minute or two until they were ready to ride into the ring, Lani cleared her throat and went on.

"Everyone who's ever seen a rodeo knows about barrel racing," she said. "It's an exciting event for cowgirls only – no guys allowed! But that's OK, because the cowboys get to do lots of fun stuff, too, like roping and bull riding. We won't see any bulls today, but our guests are going to show you a little of pretty much everything else." She paused again, just long enough to see that Belle and Chuck were now mounted and riding toward the gate. "So without further ado, may I present to you the one and only barrel-racing superstar, Belle Carter, and the equally accomplished reiner and roper, Chuck Braxton! Let's give them a big Chestnut Hill welcome!"

The waiting crowd cheered as the couple loped

their horses into the ring. Somewhere in the bleachers below, Lani heard Dylan let out a distinctive "Whoo-hoo!"

For the next forty minutes or so, Belle and Chuck put on an impressive display of Western riding. First Chuck and his horse, Doc, gave a roping demonstration. With a radio mic fitted to his helmet, he talked about the origins of the cowboy style of riding and showed some basic roping moves, finishing up by expertly lassoing several fence posts and a dummy steer head that he'd brought with him.

Then Belle joined him in the centre of the arena, and the two of them presented a breathtaking display of trick riding, which went way beyond anything their audience would have seen in cowboy movies. They vaulted on to their saddles from the ground as their horses cantered past, then Belle hung off the horn of her saddle by one leg as Ash spun in a circle. Her stunt was almost topped when Chuck stood in the saddle and jumped rope with his lasso while Doc jogged smoothly around the ring.

When they finished, the applause was thunderous. "Ladies and gentlemen, Belle Carter and Chuck Braxton!" Lani announced, her amplified voice barely audible over the cheers and whistles.

During the show, Lani's friends had climbed up to sit next to her at the announcer's area. "Think Aunt Ali will let us try some of those tricks in our next lesson?" Dylan commented to the others.

Honey snorted. "Fat chance." She nodded toward the

ring, where Chuck was taking centre stage again. "What's he going to do next?"

"Reining, I think," Lani said, quickly consulting her notes. Then she clicked on the microphone again. "OK, everyone. Now we're going to see a demonstration of the newest international riding craze, which originated right here in the American West. Chuck will show us some of his best reining moves."

"Thanks, Lani," Chuck called, tipping his hat to her. "OK, here we go..."

He and Doc went on to demonstrate several of the basic reining patterns, explaining a little about how reining horses were trained. Lani already knew most of what he was saying, but she was really pleased to notice that her friends were watching with interest.

"Now *that* kind of stuff Ms Carmichael might let us try," Malory said, letting out an admiring whistle as Doc executed a fast, smooth rollback. "It's like the moves Lani showed us, remember?"

"Kind of," Lani admitted, watching as Doc planted his front legs in the earth and skidded forward in an impressive sliding stop. "Only this time, both horse and rider actually know what they're doing." She felt a pang as she remembered the reining moves she'd performed with Colorado. He'd showed such promise – it was too bad she wasn't able to ride him in today's activities. She pushed the gloomy thoughts away as quickly as she could, not wanting to let them spoil the day.

When Chuck finished, there was more enthusiastic applause from the crowd. He took a bow, then stepped down and looped Doc's reins over the fence. Then he hurried toward the rail to help Kelly and Sarah, who were waiting to roll the barrels into the ring and set up the course.

"Ladies and gentlemen, it's now time for our main event," Lani announced. "The barrel-racing demonstration, which will be followed by a competition open to all comers." She quickly explained the rules and rewards of the challenge.

Belle rode into the centre of the ring and explained a little about her sport. "OK, enough talking," she said after describing how she had perfected Ash's technique over several years of careful training. "Anyone ready to see some more riding?"

There was an eager cheer. Lani held her breath as Belle cantered toward the near end of the ring. She could tell Ash knew something was about to happen – the grey gelding's nostrils were flared, his steps coming quicker and choppier as he practically danced to the starting line.

Noel Cousins clambered toward the announcer's area. "You're doing awesome with the mic, Lani," she said. She glanced down at the ring, her eyes glowing. "And they're awesome, too. The crowd loves this!"

"Thanks," Lani said.

Dylan was nodding vigorously. "Yeah," she added. "Lani's doing a way better job than any Z-list celebrity Lynsey's mother might have dragged in."

Lani grinned, then spoke into the microphone. "Belle's time will be posted immediately after the demonstration is over," she said. "The competition will then be open for all challengers, so saddle up and have a go! If anyone comes within three seconds of Belle, that means even more money for AllSports, so try your best, cowgirls! Now, are we ready? Set?... GO!"

Ash leaped into a flat-out gallop, his muscles straining as he shot toward the first barrel. Lani held her breath as the grey horse spun around the barrel and burst across the ring toward the second.

"Wow!" Dylan murmured beside her.

Lani couldn't take her eyes off the pair in the ring. Belle stood in her stirrups, crouched over her horse's withers as he approached barrel number two. She sat back two strides away and Ash collected himself - underneath her, spinning around the barrel without losing any forward momentum.

"Go, Belle, go!" Lani yelled.

Ash flattened out again, racing toward the third and final barrel in the cloverleaf pattern. Once again he spun around it expertly, ending up facing back toward the finish line.

Belle flapped her arms and thumped her feet, doing everything she could to urge her horse on. The bleachers erupted as the spectators cheered them on by screaming, whistling, and stamping their feet. Barely a heartbeat later, or so it seemed, Ash sped across the finish line and pulled up, skidding into a pretty good approximation of one of the sliding stops Chuck had demonstrated a few minutes earlier. Belle was grinning from ear to ear as she leaned forward to give her horse a pat.

Lani glanced toward Noel, who was checking her cell phone. A committee member was supposed to text message them the time as soon as the timer told her.

"And the official time is—" Noel paused, then held the phone up so Lani could see the time.

"Got it," Lani said, then lifted the microphone. "OK, folks. It's official. The time to beat is fourteen point two seconds." Lowering the microphone again, she glanced over at her friends. "Wow, that's smoking," she commented as the crowd cheered Belle's brilliant effort. "Probably not the best a horse and rider like that could do on a course this size – I'm guessing Belle was being nice and not running Ash all out so we'd at least have a shot at that prize – but it's still going to be awfully hard to beat."

"Don't worry," Dylan assured, cracking her knuckles. "Just wait until Morello and I get out there and show them how it's done."

Despite Dylan's confidence, she and Morello didn't come anywhere close to beating Belle's time. Each horse and rider team was allowed two attempts at the barrel course, but the best Dylan could do was nineteen point six seconds.

"Oh, well," she said good-naturedly as she left the ring about twenty minutes later. "Guess Morello isn't cut out to be a barrel racer after all. Too bad you're not taking Tybalt in there, Mal – he's part Thoroughbred, right? That means he should be fast."

Lani shot Dylan a quick glance and was relieved to

see her wink, betraying that she was only joking. Malory had decided from the start that taking the sensitive, still-green pony into the barrel-racing ring was only asking for trouble. Ms Carmichael had offered to let her ride one of the other school horses, but Malory had bowed out altogether to let others have a chance to take part.

"Well, there are still plenty of people lined up to give it a shot," Lani said, nodding toward the horses and riders milling around outside the ring. "I don't think Belle should put away her cheque book just yet!" Suddenly she couldn't bear to watch anyone else tackle the barrel—racing course, not when all she could think of was how brilliantly Colorado had run over Ms Carmichael's course a few weeks before. Making an excuse to the -others that she had an errand to run – which wasn't unconvincing, given her hectic schedule so far that day – she left them hanging over the rail to watch the next competitor and fled into the crowd.

A couple of hours later, Lani had pitched in to help members of the Food Committee count the ballots for the chili cook-off, reunited a lost toddler with his anxious mom, and taken a turn at the ticket booth by the carnival games. By the time Wei Lin arrived to take over at the ticket booth, with Honey tagging along, Lani realized the Rodeo Day was nearly over and her sister still hadn't turned up.

"What's the matter?" Honey asked when she saw Lani's face.

"It's Marta." Lani checked her watch for the umpteenth time. "I just don't understand why she's not here yet." She hoisted the heavy board blocking the back entrance to the booth, holding it up so Wei Lin could duck inside to take her place.

"Are you sure she's not here somewhere?" Wei Lin asked as she sat down in the folding chair. "With all these zillions of people, she might still be looking for you in the crowd."

Lani hadn't thought of that. "I guess you're right," she said. "I'll just feel better when I see her." She sighed. "I wish I'd thought to borrow someone's cell so she could just call me…"

Wei Lin already had a line of customers waiting to buy tickets for the games, so she merely shot Lani a sympathetic smile before starting to count out change.

"Come on," Honey said. "Let's go find the others. Maybe they can help you look for Marta."

"OK," Lani said. "Wei Lin's probably right – she could have been here for hours without us running into each other." They headed toward the main ring. "By the way, how's the barrel-racing challenge going?" she forced herself to ask. "Anybody win yet? I couldn't hear the announcements very well from the ticket booth."

"I'm not sure," Honey said. "I haven't heard Noel announce a winner. But I got distracted by the funnel cake stand so I might have missed it. Those cakes are totally delicious! We don't have them in England, you know. I wish I could save one for Sam."

"Trust me, they don't keep well," Lani warned.

"Although that might be because they're too darn tempting! Come on, let's go find out what's happening."

They soon spotted Dylan and Malory leaning against the rail near the ring's main gate. The feisty part-Thoroughbred gelding, Prince of Thieves, was in the process of knocking over the second barrel while his owner, Granville junior Anita Demarco, tugged helplessly at the reins.

"Anyone win the prize yet?" Lani asked. It wouldn't be poor Anita, who was racking up a score of penalty points as Prince sidestepped restlessly toward the third barrel.

"Not even close," Dylan said grimly. "The best time so far is eighteen three."

"Do you think there's any chance Belle would stretch it out to five seconds instead of three?" Malory wondered. "I'd hate to think of AllSports not getting the extra cash just because we can't ride fast enough."

"I don't know – we agreed to three seconds, so I think we have to stick to that," Lani said. "Did you have a turn yet, Honey?"

Honey nodded. "Falcon and I were pretty feeble," she admitted. "The first time, we got confused and turned the wrong way around the third barrel. The second time we made it through, but our time was about twenty-five seconds."

"Twenty-seven point two," Dylan corrected with a grin. "Let's be accurate here."

Honey stuck out her tongue at Dylan. "Nice talk from another loser," she joked.

Just then Ali Carmichael stepped into the middle of the ring holding a microphone, accompanied by Belle Carter. The riding director glanced over her shoulder at Kelly and Sarah, who were resetting the barrel Prince had knocked over.

"OK, people," she said. "We've had a lot of tries so far, but Belle Carter's challenge still stands. Are you telling me we don't have anyone here who can come close to her time?"

The crowd hooted good-naturedly as Belle grinned and held out her arms, openly inviting challengers. But nobody stepped forward to take a turn. Most of the ponies were already back in the barn or their pastures; the only people still mounted were Lynsey, who was sitting on Bluegrass a few yards away, and Nadia, who was standing next to her on Hardy.

Following Lani's gaze, Malory shook her head. "They both went already," she said. "Bluegrass did pretty well on his second try – nineteen point eight. To be honest, I think Lynsey would have been horrified if he'd got any closer. She's terrified he's a secret cow pony!"

Grinning, Lani scanned the crowd for other possible competitors. Somehow, she'd assumed all along that someone would be able to make the time and win that money.

Chuck was striding out to join Ali in the ring. He took her microphone and addressed the crowd. "Come on, folks!" he called out. "My girlfriend here can't ride *that* fast. Besides, if y'all let her win this, there'll be no livin' with her for the rest of this trip. So come on, someone take pity on a poor cowboy and get out here and whup her time!"

"You know, that guy might be a hick," Nadia commented from atop her horse, just loudly enough for Lani and her friends to hear, "but he sure knows how to wear a pair of jeans."

Lani hid a grin as Lynsey, still sitting atop Bluegrass beside Nadia, let out a snort. "Well," Lynsey said after a pause, "I suppose you may have a point. Those chaps would be a hideous fashion disaster on most people, but he sort of carries them off, doesn't he?"

Lani was still smiling over that when Honey nudged her in the side. "Don't you think it's time you went and tacked up Colorado now?" she asked softly.

Lani raised her eyebrows. "What are you talking about? You know I can't ride yet." She gestured toward her sling.

"Don't give me that." Honey shook her head. "I saw you just now lifting up that board at the ticket booth. It didn't look like your wrist was giving you any trouble then."

"Oops." Lani glanced over to make sure Dylan and Malory weren't listening. Luckily they were deep in conversation with some girls on their other side. "I guess you caught me," she admitted sheepishly.

Honey looked puzzled. "Why are you pretending your wrist still hurts?"

Lani rubbed her forehead. "It's kind of complicated," she began.

"Come on, spill it," Honey ordered. "We're best

friends, right? That means we tell each other everything."

"You're right. Sorry." Lani took a deep breath. "If you really want to know, I reckoned my wrist was the best excuse I had for not riding."

"But why wouldn't you want to ride?" Honey searched her face with troubled blue eyes. "Did the fall shake you up? Are you afraid to get back on?"

"No! Nothing like that." Lani shook her head. "It's just – I thought maybe if I gave up riding, my folks might be more likely to let me stay. And if I don't get to stay, then Colorado won't miss me so much if I haven't been around all term." The confession came out in a rush and Lani paused for breath, wondering if Honey would think she was a total idiot.

"Oh!" Honey's eyes widened with sudden understanding, and nothing but sympathy. "Wow, that's rough. Do you really think you might have to give up riding if you stay?"

"I don't know," Lani admitted. "I mean, planning this fund-raiser has been a ton of work, so I haven't had enough time to study as hard as I meant to, even with you guys helping me." She shrugged. "What difference does it make, anyway? There's no way I could take part in the barrel racing, even if I hadn't been wearing this stupid sling. It's ages since I've been on a horse, and I missed most of the practices."

"Don't be ridiculous," Honey chided her. "You and Colorado were brilliant that very first day, and you hadn't had any practice then, either."

"I guess. But if my parents hear I'm riding again—"

"There's no point hiding away your talents in the hope of pleasing your parents," Honey said, speaking more sharply than usual. "You're only hurting yourself. Would your dad and mum really want that?"

Lani hadn't thought about it that way. "I guess not," she admitted, picking at a splinter on the rail in front of her. "They only want what's best for me. Dad said that in his letter."

"There you are, then. And what's best for you right now is to get out there and prove that Belle isn't the only fabulous barrel racer here!" Impulsively, Honey reached out and gave Lani a big hug. "You've done an incredible job running this event, but you need to stay true to who *you* are. And that means riding Colorado, as best as you can. Now go for it!"

Lani hugged her back, a little surprised by the gesture. While Honey was one of the most kindhearted and loving people Lani knew, she wasn't usually so demon-strative.

"Well, if you insist," Lani said, anticipation already building up inside her. She looked down at the sling on her wrist. "But what's everyone going to say when—"

"Never mind about that. We can explain everything later." Honey grabbed Lani's free hand and pulled her toward the barn entrance. "Come on, I'll help you tack up – I'm practically an expert at tying those Western girths now!"

Chapter Twelve

Dylan and Malory looked utterly confused when Lani appeared leading Colorado in full Western tack, but when she promised to explain later, and Honey told them to just shut up and cheer, they shrugged and went along with it.

In the ring, Ms Carmichael had taken back the microphone from Chuck. "OK, folks, this is your last call," she was saying. "Do we have any more takers? Five, four, three, two…"

"Wait!" Lani called, opening the gate. "I want to try, please."

Ms Carmichael looked surprised. Lowering the microphone, she stepped over to Lani. "Are you sure?" she asked. "Your wrist—"

"My wrist has been fine for weeks." Lani had left her sling in the barn. Now she raised her arm and wriggled her hand, proving she had a full range of movement. "I just – I just wasn't sure I was ready to ride again, that's all."

Ms Carmichael nodded, seeming to understand. "All

right then," she said. Lifting the microphone again, she announced, "It looks like we have one more Chestnut Hill cowgirl willing to go for the gold! Please welcome Ms Lani Hernandez from Adams, riding Colorado."

As Lani turned to swing herself onto Colorado's back, she caught sight of a familiar face at the edge of the ring. "Marta!" she blurted out. "You made it!" She clucked to Colorado and led him over to her sister.

"Hi there," Marta said breathlessly. "I've been here for a while. Dad and I arrived together."

"Dad?" Lani froze halfway through checking her cinch. "What are you talking about?"

"That's what I'm trying to tell you," Marta said, tugging at the collar of her pink microfleece parka. "He had business in Providence this week, so he came by to visit me in Boston. When he heard I was coming down here—" She shrugged.

"Oh, no!" Lani glanced around wildly. "Help me get Colorado out of here, quick! I can't let Dad know I was going to ride."

She tugged on her pony's reins, preparing to lead him back into the barn. But Marta stretched her hand over the rail to stop her. "No!" she said. "Look, I wanted to give you the heads-up that Dad is here. But it's not bad news, Lani. He's really impressed with everything he's seen so far. The fund-raiser, I mean. Especially after someone told him you were the only seventh-grade committee head in the history of Chestnut Hill. He also ran into your principal, and she told him you're doing great so far this term academically."

"Really?" Lani said. "What did he say when he heard that?"

Marta shrugged. "Not much," she admitted. "But I could tell he was pleased. If you want a little sisterly advice, I think this might be the perfect time to show him just how important riding is to you."

Lani stood still for a moment, remembering what Honey had said a few minutes earlier. Maybe she and Marta were right. Riding was so important to her, and now that she let herself think about it, she realized just how much she'd missed it these past few weeks. Didn't her father deserve to know that about her?

Lani looked around at the people lining the bleachers, all of them enjoying Rodeo Day. It had been her idea all along, and she had done so much to make it happen. With a swelling of pride, she thought back over all the hard work that had brought them there.

If I can help organize something like this, I should be able to organize my life so I can ride and *get good marks,* she thought, with a sudden flare of optimism. *And if I can convince all these people to show up and make a donation to AllSports, surely I can work out a way to convince Dad that this is where I belong!*

"Ready to go, Lani?" Ms Carmichael asked, interrupting her thoughts.

Lani exchanged a glance with Marta, who gave her a thumbs-up. Then she took a deep breath and nodded. "I'm ready."

She was so focused on what she was about to do that she hardly heard the cheers as she swung into the saddle and jammed her feet into the stirrups. "OK, boy," she murmured, leaning forward to give Colorado a pat. "I know it's a while since we practised, but just do your best, OK?"

Colorado turned his head around and sniffed at the toe of her boot, as if wondering if it was really her up there. Lani smiled down at him, relishing the feel of being back where she belonged – on the best pony in the world. Colorado seemed to feel it, too. Sometimes he could be difficult to get going at the beginning of a ride, but today he felt fluid and willing beneath her as she headed into the centre of the ring. With Ms Carmichael's permission, she trotted him a couple of circuits to loosen him up before heading to the start line. Her three best friends hung over the rail beside the gate, along with almost a dozen of their dorm mates – Alexandra Cooper, Razina Jackson, Sydney Hunt, Wei Lin Chang, Tanisha Appleton, Carrie James, and more – all the people who had helped make Lani's Rodeo Day idea a roaring success. Even Lynsey and Nadia had joined them, still mounted on their ponies, while Patience slouched nearby against the fence.

"Go for it, Lani!" Dylan shouted.

"Bring home the money, cowgirl!" Alexandra called out, making the others laugh.

Lani lifted her eyes to search the crowd beyond her cluster of friends. It wasn't long before she spotted her father standing with Marta in the first section of bleachers. His aviator sunglasses hid his eyes, making it impossible to read his expression. But Marta was grinning broadly, and when Lani waved to them, they both waved back. She couldn't help wondering what her father was thinking as he watched her surrounded by friends and horses – the very things he was so worried about distracting Lani from her studies. Suddenly this was starting to look like a really dumb idea…

But there was no time to back out now. Noel had taken over the microphone again, quickly reminding the crowd of the rules and exactly what was at stake. "Lani is our last hope," she said. "As a reminder, Belle's time was fourteen point two. That means Lani and Colorado need to do the course in seventeen point two or better to win the challenge. Good luck, guys!"

"No pressure, right?" Lani murmured to Colorado, aiming him toward the start line.

Belle and Chuck were sitting on the fence as Lani rode past, having left Ash and Doc in the stalls for a breather after all their hard work. They waved at her cheerfully.

"Good luck, Lani!" Belle called out.

"You'll need it!" Chuck added jokingly.

"OK, Lani, now let's see what you can do," Noel said into the PA system. "Ready, set…"

As soon as Noel said "Go!", Lani dug her heels into Colorado's sides and shoved her hands forward to let him leap into motion. Colorado hurtled toward the first barrel at a flat-out gallop. But he was way too eager for Lani to have any sort of control, and he crashed into the barrel with his shoulder, sending it flying.

Lani's face flamed as she pulled him up, knowing there was no way she could beat Belle's time with a five-second penalty. "Can I go ahead and take my second turn?" she called to Ms Carmichael.

The riding director nodded, so Lani rode back to the start line while Kelly scooted into the ring to reset the barrel. Her friends were still cheering her on, but she didn't dare turn to look at them – she was afraid she might catch her father's eye by accident.

Nice way to show what a great rider you are, she thought. *He'll be really impressed by that.*

She did her best to focus on her next attempt. She couldn't give up now, not with all these people watching.

"OK, I think we're ready for Lani's second try," Noel announced. "All set, Lani?"

Afterward, Lani could barely remember taking off at the start and circling the first barrel, then the second, then the third. But she did recall feeling as if she and Colorado had never felt quite so connected – all she had to do was think of shortening his stride, collecting his hocks for the turn into the pocket, sending him off at a breakneck gallop, and he responded at once. She also remembered hearing a howl of excitement from the crowd as she and Colorado sprang away from the third barrel. And she recalled screaming his name and flapping the reins against his neck, knowing even as she did that there was no point because he was already going as fast as he could.

The faces of the spectators along the rail were

nothing but a blur as Lani and Colorado sped across the finish line. But she could definitely hear Dylan shrieking, "RIDE 'EM, COWGIRL!"

Lani grinned and pulled up, panting just as hard as Colorado. "Thank you, boy," she whispered, bending to pat him over and over. "You were amazing!"

She had no idea what her time had been, and at that moment she didn't care. It felt so good to be back in the saddle, doing what she loved, that nothing else seemed to matter.

"Do we have an official time on that run?" Noel asked. After a pause, she spoke again. "OK, here we go. As you know, the time to beat is fourteen point two, which means we're looking for seventeen point two or better to hit within that three-second mark." She paused again and glanced down. "Lani's time on her second and final run was ... seventeen point seven seconds."

There was a moment of silence. Lani slumped in the saddle. She had missed the cutoff by a half-second. *If only I hadn't messed up that first run,* she thought. *If only we still had another shot...*

"Lani!"

Glancing over her shoulder, she saw that her father and Marta had joined her friends by the rail.

Lani rode over, disappointment at her time vanishing beneath a sudden flurry of butterflies in her stomach. Was her dad going to interpret this as yet another failure? "Hey, Dad," she said. "Marta said you were here."

"And I'm glad I came!" her father exclaimed. He took off his sunglasses, and Lani saw that his eyes were dancing with pleasure. "This is a terrific event, Lani! Very, very impressive. I hear you had a lot to do with putting it together – good job! Oh, and that ride you just gave wasn't too shabby, either." He winked. "I'm glad to see you managed to stay in the saddle this time."

"Very funny, Dad. And thanks," Lani added cautiously, hardly believing her eyes and ears. "Did you really think I did OK just now?"

"Of course!" He looked surprised she doubted him. "Believe me, I've been watching your schoolmates try the same thing all afternoon. None of them could hold a candle to your ride!"

Lani grinned, already feeling as if a massive weight had been lifted from her shoulders. "Too bad we couldn't shave off another half-second, though. We just missed the cutoff for the matching funds."

Suddenly she noticed Belle Carter hurrying into the center of the ring, holding Ms Carmichael's microphone. "Listen up, everybody," Belle called, beaming around at the crowd. "I don't know if you realize it, but that was a very impressive run for an amateur." She turned to smile at Lani. "I know I said my time had to be matched within three seconds before I made a donation. But I'm so impressed by your ride that I'm going to round up. Three and a half seconds is close enough. Lani, you just won my Cowgirl Challenge!"

"Whoo-hoo!" Chuck shouted from the rail, raising

his arms above his head and clapping wildly. "That's my girl! Go, Belle!"

The rest of the crowd erupted in cheers, too. Lani stared at Belle, astonished. "Really?" she blurted out, as Chuck hopped over the fence and came toward her. "That's – that's awesome!"

A grinning Chuck offered her a bouquet of roses. "Here's your prize," he said. "We have a little something for your partner, too." He held up a "bouquet" of carrots.

Lani accepted the prizes, stammering her thanks. This was so overwhelming that it hadn't quite sunk in yet. She jumped off Colorado and fed him a couple of carrots. Then, tossing his reins and the roses to Ms Carmichael, who was smiling almost as broadly as Belle, Lani scrambled over the fence to join her friends. They were all jumping up and down and screaming with glee, and as soon as Lani's feet hit the ground, they smothered her in a giant group hug. Even Lynsey and Patience applauded.

Dr Jordan and Dr Starling joined Belle in the centre of the ring.

"On behalf of AllSports I would like to thank you so much for your generosity, Ms Carter, and all of you who have been part of the event," Dr Jordan said warmly. "I've had a fabulous time here with some of the kids who belong to the AllSports team, and we look forward to helping more kids reach their dreams in the future. Thanks for your support, everyone." Dr Jordan, who had been so poised at the symposium, looked a little overwhelmed as she handed the mic to Dr Starling.

"I'm pleased you all could join us. And, Ms Carter, I hope you're ready for the amount you're going to have to match – I have to warn you that thanks to the hard work of our Adams girls and the generosity of all our visitors, we've raised a lot of money today."

Belle put one hand over her heart, bracing herself. "OK," she joked. "What's the bad news?"

When Dr Starling gave the amount, Belle pretended to stagger backward in shock. But then she grinned and gave a thumbs-up, bringing more cheers from the crowd. "I'll be honoured to match that," she said, leaning forward to speak into the microphone. "It's been a lot of fun to be here today, and it's just great to know how many kids are going to benefit from this for a very long time."

"Wow," Lani breathed. "That really is a lot of money!"

"You bet." Dylan reached over and gave her shoulder a more restrained squeeze than her previous bear hug. "And it's mostly thanks to you. Who else would ever have come up with something like this?" She waved a hand to take in the entire Western-themed extravaganza that surrounded them.

"*That's* for sure," Lynsey commented with a touch of her usual disdain.

For some reason, seeing Lynsey purse her lips sourly in the midst of so much celebration cracked Lani up. She started giggling, then laughing out loud. Her friends joined in. Lynsey glared at them for a moment, then rolled her eyes and stalked away, leading Bluegrass behind her.

"Lani?" Commander Hernandez's voice interrupted the laughter. "Hey, cowgirl. Can I talk with you for a minute?"

Lani had been so excited, she'd forgotten her whole life was still up in the air. No matter how impressed her father had been by Rodeo Day, or her barrel-racing efforts, she was afraid she might just have proved his point – that she was too easily distracted from her studies.

"Sure, Dad," she said meekly. She glanced at her friends and gestured toward Colorado, who was still standing with Ms Carmichael. "Can you…?"

"We'll take care of him," Malory said immediately, her forehead creased with worry as she worked out what was going on. "Don't worry about a thing." The others nodded, looking just as anxious.

Lani followed her father away from the crowd. She glanced around for Marta, hoping for a little moral support. But her sister was talking to someone further down the ring, her back to Lani.

Feeling tense, Lani kept silent as her father led her to a quiet corner behind the chili stand and turned to face her. This was the moment of truth, and she wasn't sure she was ready for it.

"Well, Lani," Commander Hernandez began, rubbing his chin as he gazed at her thoughtfully, "you've really surprised me today, *chica*."

"What – what do you mean?" Lani stammered.

"When Marta told me about this Rodeo Day, I must admit, I had some reservations," he said. "It sounded like yet another distraction from your schoolwork – another confirmation that your mother and I were doing the right thing by transferring you to California."

Lani's heart seemed to freeze mid-beat. "But I've been studying really hard, too," she blurted out. "My friends have been helping me out with some subjects, and I've taken on some extra-credit stuff, and I stuck to my priorities—"

She trailed off as her father raised one hand to silence her. "I know you've put a lot of effort into your schoolwork this term, Lani," he said. "I also realize that this fund-raiser was a big project, and I know you must have worked very hard to pull it off so well." He paused for a moment, and Lani resisted the urge to yell at him, to make him get on with it, before her legs gave way completely.

"And I know as well as anyone that experiences that take place outside the classroom can be just as valuable as academic work," her father went on. "After all, colleges will want to know that you're a well-rounded person, not just all about marks."

Lani was so nervous she couldn't speak. What was he trying to say?

He didn't leave her in suspense for much longer. "What I'm getting at here, Lani, is that I'm proud of you. Really proud. That's why I'm going to tell your mother that I think we should review our decision about taking you away from Chestnut Hill."

"You mean I can stay?" Lani whispered.

Her father gazed at her seriously. "Yes, you can stay – on one condition."

Lani stared back, hardly daring to breathe. *This is it,* she told herself. *This is when he tells me I can't ride anymore. That I can stay, but only if I give up Colorado.*

"You need to keep up the good work you've started this term in your classes."

"That's it?" Lani squeaked. "Wait – you mean I can keep riding, too?"

"Of course." Her father looked surprised. "As long as it doesn't interfere with your studies." He put a hand on her shoulder. "Your mother and I always knew you loved horses, Lani. We could see that from the time you were two years old and pointing out ponies through the car windows. Not to mention all those rodeos and horse shows and riding lessons you've dragged us to over the years." He chuckled at the memories. "But until today, I didn't understand just how much riding means to you, how it makes you who you are. It's part of you, and we might as well give up and accept it." He grinned, making the corners of his eyes crinkle up. "So how about it? Do we have a deal?"

"Deal? For sure!" Lani leaped forward to fling her arms around him. She squeezed him as tightly as she could, breathing in the familiar scent of his aftershave. "Thank you, Dad. Thanks a million."

"I think you've earned it," he said, giving her another squeeze.

Pulling away, she looked around, bubbling over with her good news and eager to share. Honey, Dylan, and Malory were just heading into the barn with Colorado; Lani turned back to plant one last kiss on her father's cheek.

"I'll be right back," she promised. "I've got something very important to tell my friends."

She raced off toward the barn. When she burst in, all three of her best friends were standing in the aisle. They were clearly waiting for her, their faces tight and nervous. Even Colorado was looking over the half-door of his stall as if he knew Lani was about to say something very important.

She couldn't leave them in suspense a moment longer. "Guess what?" she yelled. "You're not getting rid of me after all. I'm staying! I'm staying!"

Lani's friends shrieked in one voice, making several horses in the barn jump and snort. But as her three best friends smothered her in the world's biggest, tightest, happiest hug, Colorado merely turned away to pull at his hay net, as if he'd known all along that this was where Lani belonged.

Have you read

Lauren Brooke's best-selling *Heartland* series?

Heartland™

Amy's Journal

An extract...

"Nine hundred! Do I hear nine hundred?" the auctioneer's voice rang out above the noise of the crowd gathered in the sales barn. Standing around a circular pen, the onlookers watched as a pretty grey filly cantered around the pen, her head high.

A young woman standing near to me and Mom held up a card with a number on.

"That's nine hundred dollars to the lady in the green coat," the auctioneer said, nodding at the woman. "Do I hear any more?"

I looked at the grey filly. Her large dark eyes were fearful, her muscles were tense. I didn't like horse sales. The horses always looked so bewildered. I tried to imagine what it must be like for them, cantering around the noisy pen, not knowing why they were there or what was happening or who all these people were.

"Any more bids, ladies and gentlemen?" the auctioneer called. There was no response. He paused and then raised his hammer. "Going, going, gone!"

I glanced at the lady. She was smiling. I hoped that she would give the filly a good home.

"Next we have Lot 122," the auctioneer called as the pen gate was opened and the filly allowed out. An old bay hunter was next in the ring. He was skinny with a sway back, but he had a noble face and wise eye. He looked round in confusion and I felt awful. He looked like he should be grazing happily in a quiet field, and now who knew what would happen to him? A lot of the horses who came to a sale would end up being sold for meat. At the thought of the fate awaiting the bay in the ring, I felt suddenly sick.

"I need to get some fresh air," I said to Mom.

She nodded. "OK, I'll meet you by the trailer in half an hour."

I pushed my way through the crowd. The barn smelled of stale sweat and horse droppings. Reaching the entrance I walked outside and breathed in deep gulps of the damp March air. It was a relief to be outside, away from the scared horses and the shouting. Mom had come to the sales to see if there were any horses who needed Heartland's help. I just wanted to take them all home.

I looked around. Nearby was a barn with a cluster of metal pens. Each pen had a pony inside, waiting for their turn in the ring. The ponies were to be sold after the horses. Prospective buyers were now walking round the concrete walkways, examining the ponies and reading the notes attached to the pen gates.

I walked over. A brown-and-white paint pony was looking over the gate of the first pen. I stroked her nose and read her notes:

Lot 244: Scout. 13.2 h.h. mare. 15 years old. Has competed in equitation and hunter pony classes. 100% to load, shoe, clip and in traffic. Ideal first pony.

Scout nuzzled my hands and I fed her a horse-cookie from my pocket.

"She'd make you a lovely pony," a man standing nearby came over. "Are you looking to buy?"

"No. . . No, I'm not," I said, and hurriedly moved on.

There were so many ponies to look at. Old and young, all different shapes and sizes from a tiny black Shetland to a handsome bay hunter pony, whose card said it had won a string of prizes in the show-ring. As I walked towards the back of the barn, I saw a group of three men standing around a pen, their arms crossed.

"Unwarranted," I heard one of the men say, shaking his head.

I went closer. I couldn't see which pony they were discussing.

"Pity. He's a good-looking animal," the third man said, going closer to the pen gate. "And young too. Feed him up and you could get a good price for him."

There was a clatter of hooves. I saw a glimpse of a golden coat and heard a clang of metal as the pony threw himself at the pen gate. All three men jumped back.

"Vicious brute!" the first man shouted, waving his arms angrily. "Go on! Get back with you!"

The pony shot to the back of his pen. Shaking their heads, the men moved away and I saw the pony for the first time

He was beautiful, a buckskin with a dirty gold coat and a tangled black mane and tail. His head was high. His ribs stuck out and there were deep grooves in his quarters, but the look in his eyes was so full of pride and spirit that it seemed to make him glow with energy. He looked around, daring the world to come near him.

My eyes went to the card on his door. There was no name. Just the words:

Lot 247: 14.2 h.h. Gelding. 9 years old. Sold unwarranted.

• • •

I looked at the pony again. I felt drawn to him, to his fire, to his spirit.

"I wouldn't go too close to that pony, honey," a voice said behind me.

I swung round. One of the men who'd been by the buckskin's pen had seen me standing there and had come back.

"He's vicious," he told me. "He just tried to take a bite out of my friend." He shook his head. "The glue factory's the only place for a creature like him. You stay away from him or you'll get hurt." He nodded, walking off.

I hesitated and then looked back at the buckskin. He had tried to attack the men – I'd seen it. But was he really vicious? He looked so beautiful.

I scanned his face. His eyes were large and set high on his face. *Intelligent eyes. Proud eyes.* The words sprang into my mind and suddenly I remembered everything Mom had been teaching me about reading horses' faces. I could hear her voice in my head: "If a horse is behaving badly then look at his face. Do his features tell you he's mean and aggressive? If not then look for another reason for his behaviour – he may be in pain, he may be scared, he may simply be misunderstood."

I started to look more closely at the shape of the buckskin's features. His wide forehead signalled intelligence. His long narrow ears suggested he might be temperamental. He had large, defined nostrils – another sign of intelligence. And just above his nostrils, he had a bump. That, combined with his high-set proud eyes suggested he was a dominant horse who needed to be treated with respect. Everything about this nameless pony suggested he was intelligent and proud. He was stubborn, but not mean – certainly not vicious.

Just then a beam of sunlight flashed through a broken slat in the barn roof and danced on the pony's golden coat. His eyes flickered to mine. Suddenly I felt a charge rush through me, and I knew that I just had to persuade Mom to buy him.

"I'll be back," I told him and, turning, I ran down the aisle.

Mom was still beside the noisy ring. "Hi," she said, looking round as I pushed my way to her side. I was out of breath and she frowned. "What's up?"

"There's a pony!" the words burst out of me. "We've got to buy him, Mom! We've just got to!"

Mom looked surprised.

"Come and see him!" I begged. "Please!"

For a moment, Mom's eyes scanned mine and then to my relief, she nodded. "OK."

I turned and began to push my way out through the crowd. "Come on!"

Mom followed me.

As we got out of the auction barn, I started to tell her about the pony. "He's 14.2 hands, a buckskin. He's being sold as unwarranted. And has a vicious reputation, and likely that he'll go for meat. But he's not mean – not deep down. I know he's not."

"You read his face?" Mom said. It was half a question, half a statement.

I nodded. "You wait till you see him," I said, heading down the aisle that led to his pen. "You'll see what I mean."

The buckskin was still at the back of the barn, standing in his pen, his head raised.

I watched Mom's face as she scanned his head.

"Potentially stubborn," she said softly. "But very bright. Proud, brave, confident, complex – a pony who needs respect."

"That's what I thought!" I said in excitement. "It's his eyes and that bump on his nose."

The pony looked at us.

Mom read the card beside him. "So you heard some people say he's vicious?"

"I saw him try and bite them," I admitted.

"Why?" Mom asked curiously.

"One of the bidders went up to the gate," I replied. I looked at her beseechingly. "Can we buy him?"

"I'm not sure yet." Her eyes fixed on the pony, Mom stepped towards the gate. The pony's ears went back. Mom stopped and turned sideways on to him. She lowered her eyes. I knew what she was doing. By turning away from him and avoiding direct eye contact, she was trying to make herself seem as unaggressive as possible. By not walking up to the gate, she was respecting his space and waiting for him to make the first move. The minutes passed. Several people came by the pen, but when they saw that the card read "unwarranted" they walked away again. It was quiet near the back of the barn and no one took any notice of what Mom was doing – no one that is, apart from the pony. He watched her intently.

The first of the ponies to be auctioned was led out of the barn by a handler. Still Mom waited. Suddenly the buckskin snorted and brought his head down slightly. Mom took a small step away from him. He lowered his head even more and stared at her.

"That's it," she whispered. "Good pony."

He took a step towards her. There was nothing fearful about him, although his eyes showed a wariness. Step by step he moved closer to the gate until he was close enough to put his head over. He snorted again and then reached out with his muzzle and touched her shoulder.

Mom stayed very still for a moment, and then raised her hand and stroked his nose.

"There," she whispered. "You're not bad, are you?"

Slowly she backed away. The pony watched her and in his eyes, I saw a glimmer of softness.

Mom looked at me. "Yes," she said. "We can bid for him. He may have his problems, but deep down I think we'll find a very good pony in there."

I was delighted. "Oh, Mom, that's great! You really think we can help him?"

"No, but I think *you* can," Mom said.

I looked at her, wondering what she meant.

"You found him, Amy," Mom went on "You saw something in him that made you look beyond his behaviour. If we buy him then you should be the one to work with him."

"Me?" I stammered. I'd helped Mom with the horses, but I'd never worked with one on my own before.

Mom nodded. "You're more than ready to work with a horse on your own now, and I think this pony could be a very good starting point. I'll help you of course, but he'll be your responsibility. You can plan out his care, his training, you can work with him each day – if you want to."

I looked at the beautiful buckskin in delight. It would be like having a pony of my own. "Want to?" I exclaimed. "I'd love to!"

"Good," Mom smiled. "We'd better get ready to start bidding then."

"And now on to Lot 247," the auctioneer called. "A nine-year-old buckskin gelding. Sold unwarranted." There was the sound of shouting and the metal gate of the round pen swung open. The next instant the buckskin cantered into the ring, urged on by two handlers. Seeing the people, the pony stopped dead and pinned his ears back.

One of the handlers headed towards him. "Go on!" the man growled, swinging a rope.

The buckskin stared at him proudly and then, snaking his head down, he charged at the handler. With a yell, the man vaulted over the gate. Stopping with a defiant squeal, the buckskin stamped a front hoof down, sending a spray of sand into the air. A murmur of surprise ran through the crowd

The auctioneer cleared his throat. "So, Lot 247," the auctioneer said. "As you can see, a spirited pony. . ."

"Vicious, more like!" someone called from the crowd.

The auctioneer ignored the call. "What am I bid?"

I looked round anxiously. If the price went too high we wouldn't be able to buy the pony and right at that moment I wanted him more than anything else in the world.

The pony shook his head and squealed again.

"Who will start the bidding at six hundred dollars," the auctioneer asked.

No one in the crowd moved. Pinning back his ears the buckskin charged at the front row of people. They drew back hurriedly as he thudded into the barrier.

"Five hundred?" the auctioneer said. "Four hundred and fifty."

His voice was sounding increasingly desperate.

I glanced at the little group of meat-men. For once even their hands were still. The pony was skinny and trouble.

"Come on, ladies and gentlemen," the auctioneer encouraged. "A nice-looking pony like this. What am I bid?"

"One hundred and fifty dollars," Mom said, her voice ringing out

There was a surprised murmur. Everyone turned to look in our direction.

"One hundred and fifty dollars!" the auctioneer exclaimed. "Any advance on one hundred and fifty dollars? Look at his head, ladies and gentlemen, there's breeding in that head – he'd make a nice little pony, just needs some work. You're not seriously expecting me to sell a pony like this for one hundred and fifty."

The pony charged again at the fence and the audience gasped.

Seeming to decide that enough was enough, the auctioneer hastily brought his hammer up. "Going to the lady in the blue jacket on my left. Going, going, gone," he said, the words rushing out of him as he banged the hammer down to close the sale. The clerk wrote down Mom's number and I hugged Mom in delight. The pony was mine!

It took four handlers to get the pony out of the ring and back into his pen. Mom went to the office and paid and we fetched a halter from the trailer. "I want you to try and get the halter on to him," Mom said as we walked to the pen. "Just do what I did before. Stand and wait for him to make the first move."

"When do I put the halter on?" I asked.

"When you feel he's ready," Mom said.

The pony was standing at the back of the pen, his body tense. We stopped a couple of metres away from his gate. He stared at us and then snorted. It was as though he recognized us.

I walked forward and, hiding the halter in one hand, did just what Mom had done. Within ten minutes, the pony had come to the gate and was standing with his nose by my shoulder. "Here," Mom said, slipping a small tin into my free hand.

It was a tin of her special powder that she made from herbs and old bits of chestnut – the horny growths on the inside of horses' legs. I had seen her use it with new horses many times. It calmed them down.

Moving slowly so as not to alarm the pony, I eased the lid off the tin and rubbed a little of the gritty grey powder on to my hands, then I held out my palms towards the buckskin. He snuffed at them and then lifting his muzzle to my face, he breathed out. I breathed in his sweet hay-scented horsy breath and breathed out softly. He snorted and lowered his head.

I slowly lifted the halter and fastened it on to his head. All the time his dark eyes watched me but, to my relief, he accepted my touch. I unbolted the gate.

"We're going to take you home now," I said.

"Ask him to come with you, Amy, don't tell him," Mom said quickly. "He's got to feel you respect him. If he feels that, I'm sure he'll do what you want."

"Shall we go to the trailer?" I asked the pony.

He looked at me for a long moment with unblinking dark eyes and then he stepped forward and followed me out of the pen. As we walked up the aisle, I felt people looking at us and nudging each other. Clearly everyone was stunned by the change in him.

Smiling to myself I led the pony out of the barn and over to our trailer. Without hesitating, he followed me up the ramp and inside.

"Well done," Mom said, putting up the ramp and coming round to the jockey door. I looked round and seeing the pride in her eyes, I felt suddenly warm.

"So what are you going to call him?" she asked, as I got out of the trailer.

I thought for a moment and glanced back inside at the buckskin, who was now pulling at a haynet. Suddenly I remembered how, in the barn, the sun had streamed in through a gap in the roof and danced on his golden coat.

"Sundance," I replied.

A must-have companion book
to the *Heartland* series.

Amy's Journal

Share Amy's memories of the people and horses who inspire her in her own personal diary. Learn the techniques and remedies used at Heartland, find out how to read a horse's character from his face, and take an exclusive peek at Amy's collection of newspaper cuttings, notes and favourite family recipes.

Healing horses, healing hearts. . .